FROZEN PEACHES

PICK UP MORE PEACH ADVENTURES!

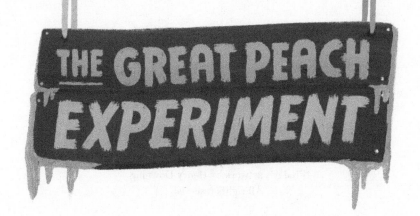

FROZEN PEACHES

ERIN SODERBERG DOWNING

PIXEL✚INK

PIXEL✛INK

Pixel+Ink is an imprint of TGM Development Corp.
www.pixelandinkbooks.com
Printed and bound in February 2023 at Maple Press, York, PA, U.S.A.
Book design by Michelle Cunningham

Cataloging-in-Publication information
is available from the Library of Congress.

Hardcover ISBN: 978-1-64595-135-3
E-book ISBN: 978-1-64595-137-7

First Edition

1 3 5 7 9 10 8 6 4 2

For Bethany and Alison
(and the rest of the fun crew at Pixel+Ink),
who have helped turn my Peach experiment
into a truly marvelous adventure.

1

SWEEPSTAKES SURPRISE

Freddy Peach had been keeping a *huge* secret from his family, and it was finally time to spill the beans. "Everyone, I have an announcement," just-turned-eleven-year-old Freddy blurted out at dinner one evening, a few weeks before spring break. Then he sat quietly and waited for their full attention. The trouble was, Freddy made *many* announcements—most of which were interesting random facts he'd recently learned—and the rest of his family sometimes ignored him. He cleared his throat and added, "An *important* announcement."

Twelve-year-old Lucy grabbed a roll from the plate in the center of the table and began to butter it. "Freddy, you already told us that bees can only produce about a teaspoon of honey in their entire lifetimes." She turned to their younger brother, Herb, and asked, "Can you please pass the milk?"

Herb, who was eight (but almost nine), set down his fork and carefully slid a carton of milk across the giant wooden table that filled the center of their family's large and formal dining room. "And we also know that a queen bee can lay up to two thousand eggs in a day." Herb popped a piece of curly pasta in his mouth and chewed thoughtfully. "That's more than one egg per minute!"

"This isn't a bee announcement," Freddy clarified.

Their dad, Walter, stood up to get himself some sparkling water from the fridge in the kitchen, then returned to his spot at the head of the table. "We have just one family of four checking into the bed-and-breakfast tomorrow," Dad blurted out, continuing to ignore Freddy's announcement. "I was thinking we could let them spread out into *both* of the guest rooms on the second floor, since no one else is staying with us at The Peachtree B and B this weekend."

The Peach family had recently opened a bed-and-breakfast in an old, historic mansion in their hometown of Duluth, Minnesota. They had spent several months fixing up their Great Aunt Lucinda's former house and had opened their doors to the public just after

Thanksgiving. There were three guest rooms at the B&B in total, but ever since Christmas had come and gone, these guest rooms stood empty most of the time.

Though Duluth was a beautiful city nestled right at the very tip of Lake Superior in Minnesota, it was freezing cold most of the winter, and not a lot of people wanted to visit. The Peaches were hoping business would pick up a bit come summer, because the mansion was an awfully big house for just the four of them. And, in order to continue to be able to afford to pay all the expensive heating and electric bills that came along with living in a house like this, Dad had told them they really needed more customers.

"That's a good idea to let the guests spread out, Dad," Lucy agreed. "I'm sure they'll be much more comfortable in two rooms than they would be in one room with a couple of fold-up beds crammed in. We can hope for a great review online after they stay!"

Freddy cleared his throat.

"How old are the kids who are coming this weekend?" Herb asked. "Where do they live?"

Lucy added, "Are they coming to Duluth for an event, or to ski, or—"

"WHY IS EVERYONE IGNORING MY

IMPORTANT ANNOUCEMENT?" Freddy shouted, interrupting his sister. The other three members of the Peach family turned to look at him. Freddy nodded. Much better. "Hello, family. Now that I have your attention," he said, "I have something very exciting to share with all of you."

"There's been an awful lot of lead-up to whatever it is you're about to say," Lucy muttered. "This better be a good announcement."

Lucy made a fair point, but Freddy ignored the jab. "Do you want the good news or the *very* good news first?"

Herb squeezed his eyes closed, then blurted out, "Start with the regular good news."

"Thanks to good ol' Freddy Peach, everyone's favorite brother and son," Freddy said with a flourish, "we have won . . . a whole year's supply of yogurt!"

Dad blinked. "What, now?"

"A whole *year's* worth of yogurt," Freddy said with a mile-wide grin. "For us, for free." Before anyone had a chance to ask any more questions, Freddy explained. "Over the past couple of months, I've been entering Dad in dozens of sweepstakes and contests."

"*Me?*" Dad said.

"You have to be eighteen to win most sweepstakes,"

Freddy explained. "So I've been using your name and birthdate. And a fake email address I set up with Theo's help, so you wouldn't get a bunch of junk emails in your regular account." Theo was the guy their family had hired to help at the B&B whenever Dad was at work and the Peach kids were at school. He was also a counselor at the Cardboard Camp that Freddy went to each summer, which made him one of the coolest people on earth.

"Ah—" Dad said, covering his mouth to hide a bubbly-water burp.

"Anyway," Freddy went on. "I felt like luck has finally been on our side lately, so I decided to enter us in some sweepstakes to test my theory."

Up until about nine months ago, things in the Peach house hadn't been so great. After Freddy's mom died a couple years ago, their family sort of fell apart. Dad disappeared into his work, they never had time or energy for fun as a family, and the world felt all wrong without Mom in it anymore. But last spring, one of Mom's inventions had sold and Dad used part of the money to buy a food truck so the four Peaches could travel around the country baking and selling pies. After they came home from that road trip, Great Aunt Lucinda had given them her mansion, and they'd somehow managed to turn her old *Peach Pit* into the all-new *Peachtree B&B*. Life still didn't feel *right* without Mom in it, but at least everything didn't feel quite as *wrong* anymore.

"I entered us in every single sweepstakes and contest I could find online and in magazines—the ones that looked legit, anyway—and we won!" Freddy grinned.

"Yogurt," Lucy repeated blandly.

"Yogurt," Freddy agreed, nodding. "A whole year's worth of yogurt!"

Dad slapped the table. "Well, that *is* good news." Then he frowned and said firmly, "It's not okay that you impersonated me to enter a bunch of sweepstakes, and I'll need to talk to Theo about the whole fake email thing . . . but it's pretty neat that you—uh, *I*—actually won something."

"I also entered you in a contest to win a lifetime supply of coffee and free breakfast at the New Scenic Café. I signed up for a cheese contest and entered to win the chance to get bread-baking lessons from a French chef..." Freddy was having a hard time remembering all the sweepstakes he'd entered but rattled off a few that popped into mind. "A free cookie-of-the-month subscription! Um, a trip to visit the set of a soap opera, a walk-on role in a Nickelodeon show, family season passes for a minor league baseball team in Kansas—"

"I always thought sweepstakes like that were fake," Herb interrupted. "I assumed no one ever won."

"Me too!" Freddy said. "But *we* won. A whole year's worth of yogurt. Do you think they deliver it all at once, or do you think it comes in the mail every few weeks? Do you think we get to *pick* the flavors we want, or will they just mail us a random selection and we'll be stuck with, like, fourteen cof-fee-and-cream flavor yogurts that no one wants to eat? I won-der if—"

Lucy cut him off. "Wait . . . you said this was the *good* news. What's the *very* good news? Are we getting a year's supply of granola to go *with* the yogurt?" She bit her lip hopefully. "Or a walk-on role in the Nickelodeon show?"

Freddy shook his head. "Nope, even better."

"Spill it," Lucy said.

"We also won . . ." Freddy paused, for dramatic effect. "A *trip* to . . ."

Dad, Lucy, and Herb all stared at him. The only sound in the dining room was the snuffling and smacking sound of the family's four small dogs chewing bits of food that had mysteriously "fallen" off Herb's plate and onto the floor.

"Ladies and gentlemen, buckle your seat belts and zip up your coats! The Peach family will soon be on our way to one of the most famous tourist destinations in the world, because we've won . . ." he said, dangling his secret news before them like a wrapped gift. Finally, Freddy hollered out, "We've won a trip to the world-famous Icehotel in Sweden!"

The dogs all began barking like crazy, sharing in his excitement.

"To an . . . ice hotel?" Dad echoed. "Did I hear that correctly?"

"You heard right," Freddy said, pounding his fists on the table. "Get ready, Peaches, because we're going to Sweden!"

From the Sketchbook of Freddy Peach:

B&B ADVERTISING IDEAS

COME TO
THE PEACH PIT

**Try our peaches!
They're not as
fuzzy as they look!**

It's like cereal!!!

Now Offering:
World's Largest Bowl
of Cereal!*

*World's Largest Bowl Not
Always Available

2

ACROSS THE OCEAN

The next few weeks at The Peachtree B&B were very busy and action-packed. But as Herb Peach knew all too well, his family had gotten pretty good at handling chaos. In the past eight or nine months alone, they had opened (and then sold) a food truck business, opened (and fixed up) a mansion bed-and-breakfast, and now they'd been tasked with packing and getting everything ready at the B&B so they could take a big family trip to Sweden.

Herb had never been to Sweden. In fact, he didn't know *anyone* who had been to Sweden. That's part of what made this sweepstakes prize that Freddy had won for them so exciting. It was fun doing things other people had not! This would be *another* Great Peach Experiment for Herb's family . . . but this time, the experiment sounded less like hard work and more like a whole lot of fun!

It had been a lot of crazy days in a row, and a lot of hard waiting, but they'd finally gotten everything ready and packed and planned, and now they were at the ginormous Minneapolis airport waiting for a flight to the other side of the world. "Security is over here," Dad said, gesturing toward a long line of people. "Does everyone have their passports and tickets ready?"

Herb patted his backpack, which was strapped to his front rather than his back. He wanted to be certain he didn't lose anything that was tucked inside, and worried that wearing the pack on his back would make him nervous about someone stealing his things. He zipped open the front pocket and peeked inside; his passport and boarding pass were right where he'd put them.

"Ready, Dad!" Herb replied, proud to have been trusted to hold on to all his own stuff. Herb's stuffed pig was nestled inside the bigger

section of his pack along with Lucy's stuffed duck. He had also packed a toothbrush for the morning (they would be flying *overnight*, and he didn't want to start the day with furry teeth!), and a picture of his four little dogs so he wouldn't miss them as much, and a pair of headphones to watch movies on the plane. He'd also snuck in a comfy, fluffy pair of sock-slippers to change into while he slept. It felt funny to think about sleeping while sitting up, wearing all his clothes instead of jammies, but Lucy had told him that was how it worked with international flights.

Herb was still having a hard time believing they were taking a flight to a whole other country. A flight across the giant ocean! A flight that was going to last the entire night long!

At first, right after Freddy had told the family about their grand prize sweepstakes win, Dad had been a little nervous about the idea of a trip to Sweden because it was hard for him to take so much time away from work, and this would be the longest they'd ever been away from the B&B.

He was also worried because it sounded expensive. As it turned out, the prize package included airfare and a week's stay at the Icehotel, but there was one little catch: They had to take their trip at a very specific time. Apparently, the sweepstakes Freddy had entered them in was a contest specifically for small bed-and-breakfast and inn owners, sponsored by the North American Bed-and-Breakfast Association. The purpose of the prize was to give small, specialty hotel owners (like the Peaches!) a chance to come together to learn about running a successful tourist hotel from the best of the best. The Icehotel was world-famous, and they obviously did many things very well—since the frozen hotel was booked solid every single night of every single year.

All the grand-prize winners of the sweepstakes had been invited to come stay at the same time—which was, luckily, during the week of Herb, Lucy, and Freddy's spring break. The Peaches would be staying at the frozen wonderland in the north of Sweden with all the *other* sweepstakes winners. Herb thought it felt kind of like the kids who had won a trip to the chocolate factory in the book *Charlie and the Chocolate Factory.* Hopefully, no one would turn into a blueberry or get sucked into a TV or a chocolate river, like in the book and movie versions of Roald Dahl's Wonka story. But while they were there, Freddy had told Herb and Lucy that there would be some sort of Frozen Olympics taking place, and they—the Peaches!—would get to participate in this weeklong contest as a family. Herb really hoped they would win, whatever the prize was. It felt good to be a winner.

Even though the Icehotel adventure they were going on was free, Dad still hadn't been easily convinced to accept their prize. "It's *Sweden*," he'd kept muttering, even though that was obvious. "It's *cold* there. And very far away."

"Dad, we live in Duluth, Minnesota," Lucy had kept reminding him. "It's cold here, too."

"It's a hotel made of *ice*," Dad had said, his fingers twisting together into a nervous knot.

"Will we actually *sleep* inside a building that's all ice?" Herb had asked when Freddy was outlining all the details for them. "Or is it a regular hotel, but with ice sculptures in the lobby and icy stuff built around it and stuff?"

"I'm pretty sure we sleep inside an actual building made of ice," Freddy had replied with a casual shrug. As if sleeping inside an ice building were something totally ordinary! Herb still couldn't believe this was true, but soon he'd get to see it with his own eyes and find out how it all worked.

Eventually, once he confirmed the trip would cost them no money at all and after he was able to convince their hotel manager, Theo, to keep an eye on the B&B

for the week, Dad agreed that they could accept the grand prize. But this decision *also* came after he had a chance to speak with some scientists he knew who did research like Dad's, except they did their work in Sweden. Dad was a scientist, and he studied climate and ocean cores and soil and other stuff like that. After talking with a few researchers in Sweden, he'd happily announced to his family, "I've been in touch with a team of scientists that works out of the town the Icehotel is in. And they've invited me to visit their glacial research station with them while we're there!"

After *that* good news, everything was officially settled.

Since Dad was planning to do a bit of work during their trip, he'd suggested that they invite Great Aunt Lucinda along on their adventure as a second adult. Because she was the whole reason they got to live in The Peachtree B&B in the first place, Herb and his siblings agreed that she should get to enjoy the prize, too. Great Aunt Lucinda was always up for an adventure, so she immediately said yes and started packing.

In just a matter of days, they had booked flights, applied for rush passports for Herb and his siblings, and convinced Theo to also take care of Herb's four naughty dogs while they were out of the country. They didn't have any guests booked to stay at the B&B during the next couple of weeks, anyway, so Freddy kept insisting this was as good a time as any for a frozen family business trip.

Now, several weeks and a lot of packing and preparing later, Dad was fumbling with his backpack, trying to find his own passport—which was buried among a whole bunch of work papers inside. Lucy was reading while they shuffled forward in the long, slow security line, and Freddy was busy watching people. Herb knew his older brother would probably spend much of their flight drawing silly versions of many of these people in his sketchbook; Freddy loved studying people in real life and then making up a fictional name and backstory for them later.

"Is my hair straight?" Great Aunt Lucinda asked Herb quietly as the five Peaches moved in a herd toward the ID and security checkpoint with all the other air travelers.

Herb studied his great aunt's face and hair carefully. Great Aunt Lucinda wore a wig most days, which meant her hairstyle always changed with her mood. She had countless numbers of wigs, and for their flight to Sweden, she'd selected a black-and-gray speckled one that Herb didn't like all that much. The front of the wig looked like a smooth shark fin that draped across her forehead and cheek at a sharp angle. It made her look much sterner and grouchier than she actually was. "It's a little bit crooked," Herb whispered. "But I think it's supposed to look like that?"

Great Aunt Lucinda took a selfie with her cell phone's camera and studied the picture. She reapplied lipstick, pursed her lips, and took another photo. With a satisfied nod, she then pasted the selfie into a text message and forwarded it to her best friends at the Birch Pond retirement community. "Gotta tell the girls I'm on my way," she told Herb. "I hope you know how much they're all going to miss you this week."

Herb had been working as a helper at Birch Pond for the past six months, keeping the plants watered, the fish and turtles fed, and he also did small chores for some of the residents who lived there. During his shifts, he also spent time visiting with Great Aunt Lucinda and her friends. His job made him feel useful, in a way that he often *didn't* feel useful at the B&B. There were a lot of tasks that had to get done around their giant mansion to keep it comfortable for their guests, and most of them were not things Herb could do. Dad often reminded Herb that taking care of the dogs was a very important job that he excelled at, but sometimes Herb wished he could be trusted with a little more responsibility, like his older siblings. Freddy got to help cook and serve their guests, and he did some of the little repairs that needed doing around the house. Lucy was in charge of making sure the guest rooms were well-stocked with shampoo, lotion, and other items, and she also helped manage the guest book and made activity and dinner reservations for their guests. Maybe Herb would learn some things at the Icehotel in Sweden that he could use to help out more at home!

They'd reached the front of the security line, and a friendly woman in a dark uniform took their passports and tickets and studied each of them in turn. Herb did not smile because he wanted to make sure his face matched the photo inside his passport. When they had gotten their passport photos taken, Freddy told Herb he was not allowed to smile in his picture—or else. Herb wasn't sure what the "or else" could be, but he didn't want to risk it and find out. Freddy knew a lot of strange, random facts . . . so Herb had believed him. But it turned out Freddy was just kidding, and now Herb looked angry and mean inside his passport. He liked to think of himself as a friendly guy, and he didn't like that his passport told the world otherwise.

"Where you headed?" the woman asked, looking specifically at Herb.

"Sweden," Herb said.

The woman raised her eyebrows. *"Jag alskar Sverige,"* she said.

"You love Sweden?" Herb guessed she'd said.

The woman's eyebrows shot up even higher. "You speak Swedish, *lilla van*?" she asked, grinning.

"Only a little bit," Herb confessed. To prepare for their trip, he'd been doing some Swedish lessons on a language app that Lucy's friend June had told him about. But he knew enough to know that the woman had said she loved Sweden, and then called him "little friend."

The rest of Herb's family stared. He shrugged in response. It wasn't *that* weird that he'd attempted to learn the language of the country they were visiting! It was the polite thing to do, wasn't it?

After she'd checked all their documents, the woman ushered them through with a smile, a nod, and a warm "Enjoy your trip." A few minutes later they'd collected their items from the security area and were headed toward their departure gate. Once they'd found a collection of seats near each other, Lucy and Herb headed off together to try to find some food.

"I didn't know you were learning Swedish," Lucy

said, wrapping her hand through his. Herb liked to hold hands with his big sister; it made him feel safe. He wasn't often in places as crowded as the Minneapolis airport, and he worried about getting swept away with the crowd. But Lucy's hand tied him to something familiar, and that helped make him more confident. Lucy was good at making Herb feel better most of the time; she took care of him a lot after their mom had died.

Herb swung their hands forward and backward through the air as they walked. "I am," Herb said. "I've been using that app your friend June has. The one her dads made her use all last summer to practice her Spanish every day."

"Huh," Lucy said, sounding surprised. "Good for you."

They got burgers and fries from McDonald's, which was the cheapest dinner option, and then rejoined the rest of the family near their airplane's gate. By the time Dad, Great Aunt Lucinda, and Freddy all got food and went to the bathroom, it was time for them to board their flight. They would be flying all night long to Amsterdam, in the Netherlands, and then they'd get on *another* flight to Stockholm, Sweden. From there, they would get on a *third* flight to a small town called

Kiruna, in the north of Sweden. Then they would get to ride in a van to the Icehotel.

Herb was so excited that he wasn't sure he would be able to sleep. He'd been in an airplane before, for one of Dad's science conferences, but he had never flown to another country. Herb, Lucy, and Freddy were sharing a row in the middle of the plane. Herb called dibs on the seat in the very middle, right between his two older siblings. Dad and Great Aunt Lucinda were in a section of two seats just across the aisle from them.

The seat in front of Herb had a little TV mounted to the back, and there were hundreds of movies and shows to choose from. Herb spent time studying everything, and before long, the plane was full and they had soared into the air.

"Would you like something to drink?" A friendly man in a snazzy uniform leaned toward Herb with a smile. "Soda, juice, water?"

"Yes, please," Herb said.

"Which one, hon?" the man asked.

"Can I have all of them?" Herb asked.

The man laughed, and Lucy leaned in to tell him he was supposed to just pick one drink, not all of them. Herb was embarrassed, but the man didn't seem to care that he'd broken the rules. Uniform Man quickly filled three cups—one with Sprite, one with apple juice, and one with ice water. Herb waited for him to hand them out to him and his siblings, but he'd poured them *all* for Herb! Herb had three drinks all to himself. Then the man handed him a packet with cheese-flavored crackers, and another with warm cookies, and a third with salted almonds. Flying across the ocean was wonderful!

While Herb ate, he glanced over Freddy's shoulder at his brother's sketchbook. Freddy had decided to create a sketchbook journal of their trip, full of all the people and things they saw and met along their journey. He'd also started designing some advertising posters and billboard ideas for The Peachtree B&B, since the Peaches had been trying to come up with ideas for how to get more customers to stay at the mansion. So far, Freddy's advertising ideas were all a little strange—and some were downright scary—but they made Herb giggle.

Once the sky outside the airplane had turned dark, they were served a yummy meal of soft pasta and cold rolls with butter and a salad with exactly one tiny tomato on top of it. After his second dinner, Herb stumbled down the aisle of the airplane to visit the bathroom and brush his teeth, then changed into his comfy socks and snuggled up with his and Lucy's stuffed duck and pig. He turned on a movie he had seen many times, and as the plane gently bounced along in the air over Canada—which was somewhere way, way down below them—Herb finally fell asleep and didn't wake up until the captain announced that they were landing in Amsterdam.

From the Sketchbook of Freddy Peach:
HAPPY TRAVELERS

3

VALKOMMEN TIL SVERIGE

Standing outside the Kiruna, Sweden, airport—waiting for their van shuttle to the Icehotel to pick them up— Lucy felt like she was standing fifty feet out on a frozen Lake Superior. Icy wind whipped at her from every side, and she could feel the hairs inside her nose freeze into little crystals with each breath in. She tugged her fluffy plaid hat down over her ears and wrapped Herb into a tight hug between her and Dad. If they stuck together, she reasoned, maybe they would all stay a little warmer.

Every member of the Peach family was tired, cranky, and bleary-eyed—except Freddy, who had slept marvelously on the plane and was now *so* excited about everything new that Lucy wondered if he'd ever sleep again. Their flights had all landed on time, but they'd been traveling all night and for the better part of the next day. And besides Freddy, none of them had slept well in the airplane.

Dad had worked for much of the flight, reading journal articles and research papers that the scientists he would be meeting with had sent to him to prepare for his visit to the research station beside a glacier in the north of Sweden. This turned out to be a good thing, because when Dad *did* fall asleep, just a few hours before they landed in Amsterdam, he had snored—loudly. Last summer, when they'd been camping in tents during their food truck adventure and could hear *everything* around them all night long, the three Peach kids had dealt with more than their fair share of Dad's nighttime honking. Lucy had almost forgotten about Dad's snoring, now that they lived in the Peach Pit and his bedroom was a floor below hers. She hadn't missed hearing *that* awful sound in the night.

Great Aunt Lucinda had swapped wigs at some point during their journey, and now she was wearing the hairpiece that Freddy called the Dolly Parton (it was a big, blond, curly wig that looked just like the famous country singer's hair). She'd also slathered on gobs of lipstick and blush in the Stockholm airport bathroom, telling Lucy that a "finished face" made her feel more alive and ready to take on the day. "Even if I *feel* half dead," she'd grumbled, "at least I *look* like a million bucks. Let's all hope this hotel has a warm bed waiting for me to sink into and sleep for two days."

The Icehotel's shuttle driver was a jolly, round man named Josef (according to the patch sewn onto his chest), who was bundled up in a giant yellow snowsuit and fluffy boots. Under the snowsuit and layers of warm clothes, it was entirely possible Josef was actually the size of Herb; but it was hard to tell what a person looked like under all those puffy layers. "Hey, hey, Peaches!" Josef called out, reaching for Great Aunt Lucinda's large suitcase first. *"Valkommen til Sverige!* Welcome to Sweden!"* He swung Great Aunt Lucinda's case up and into the van, then followed with the rest of the family's bags. While the Peaches all shuffled into the old, clanky beast of a van that reminded Lucy a whole lot of the food truck they'd owned the previous summer, Josef continued to yammer away in nearly perfect English.

In fact, Lucy realized, almost *everyone* they'd spoken to so far in Sweden had only the tiniest trace of an accent. Now, Lucy felt kind of guilty that Herb was the only one in the family who had tried to learn the *Swedes'* language; they were the guests in their country, after all . . . why should their hosts be forced to talk to them in English? What if Lucy and her family had to greet all of *their* guests at The Peachtree B&B in the guests' native language? It would be a wonderful and welcoming thing to do, sure, but it also seemed impossible. Did Josef also speak Mandarin, and Spanish, and Urdu, and every other language on earth? Probably not. But he was an expert at English, that was for sure.

"We have just a short ride to get to the Icehotel," Josef explained as the van rattled to life and he began the drive away from the small airport. "We'll get you checked in to one of the rooms in our property's warm hotel for tonight, so you can settle into bed a little earlier and get a good night's rest. But then tomorrow night you will be getting to spend the night sleeping in one of our Ice Suites in the Icehotel itself!"

"Is it actually made of—" Herb began, but Josef cut him off, pointing out this and that as they drove along the snow-covered roadway. Lucy knew her brother wanted to know if the hotel was made of ice, and she did, too. She couldn't wait to see how this whole thing worked!

Lucy tried to take everything in, but she was so tired that she found herself zoning out and was only dragged out of her half sleep when Josef pumped on the brakes to let a sled pulled by dogs cross the road in front of them.

"Sled dogs!" Herb yelped.

"Are you a musher, little man?" Josef asked. "Do you like to go dogsledding?"

"Yes, I love it," Herb said, which couldn't be true since they'd never even *been* dogsledding. Lucy could tell her little brother immediately felt guilty for the lie, since he quickly changed his answer to: "I mean, I would like to try it, but I've never done it before."

"We can change that," Josef said with a laugh. "I can teach you." Then, not realizing he'd just made Herb's whole year with that promise, Josef continued to talk about food, animals, the history of the Icehotel, and told stories of the artists who had helped design that year's structure.

Freddy knotted his eyebrows together. "What do you mean, '*this* year's structure'? Does the hotel change much from year to year?"

"It changes very much," Josef said. "Of course, we have a normal, warm hotel on our property that is not made of ice, for the guests who prefer to sleep in a warm bed. That hotel doesn't change. But then we also have the Icehotel, which is built entirely of ice and all the furniture and art inside are *also* made of ice. Each spring, the Icehotel melts and returns itself to the river Torne. That's where we harvest the ice we use to rebuild the Icehotel each fall. We bring in artists from all over the world to help design Ice Suites inside the hotel that are one-of-a-kind and only last for one winter. Then next year, we begin it all again."

"Can I design a room?" Freddy asked. "I've designed a treehouse before."

"Would you like to learn to carve ice?" Josef asked him.

Freddy's eyes bugged out of his head. "Um, yes?"

"I can teach you," Josef said. "I carve in my spare time."

Lucy was starting to wonder if Josef could possibly be telling the truth. How many things could he *actually* teach them to do? So far, he'd promised Herb dogsled-ding lessons and Freddy ice-carving practice. And he was also the airport shuttle driver, the hotel's welcom-ing committee, and knew the history of the Icehotel and town inside and outside. No one person could be great at all of those things on their own!

The van slowed and Lucy peered out the window to see if they were close. "There it is!" she shouted.

Her brothers, Dad, and Great Aunt Lucinda all craned their necks to see what Lucy was pointing to. As soon as the van had completely stopped, she popped open the door and rushed outside. And there it was: the world-famous Icehotel!

Huge and magnificent, the giant frozen structure towered over them like a roadside Comfort Inn—except made entirely of ice. This wasn't just a regular back-yard igloo like the ones Freddy, Lucy, and Herb some-times built with their friends after a giant snowfall in Minnesota. It was a full-scale building, with extra rooms jutting off one side, and giant front doors with mounted antlers for handles. The ice was clear in some places, white in others, and almost seemed to glow blue in others. When the setting sun's rays hit it, the whole thing sparkled like diamonds in the crisp Arctic sky. "Wow," Lucy whispered.

"Come, come," Josef said. "We'll have plenty of time to explore the Icehotel, but first, we need to get you winter-ready so you can enjoy your visit."

Lucy looked down at her Minnesota-winter coat and thick mittens and rugged boots. She *was* winter-ready. But she followed Josef into a nearby building—not one made of ice—where he stepped behind a counter and began pulling all kinds of giant snowsuits off hang-ing racks, and dug out giant pairs of boots that looked like something you might wear to walk on the moon. He grabbed bins of fluffy fur hats with flaps for ears and mittens that looked more like massive loaves of bread. On the other side of the room was a wall filled with snowshoes and skis and poles and other fun stuff.

"They provide their guests with winter clothes? And skis and snowshoes *and* ice-carving lessons?" Freddy said, gaping at Lucy. "That is a *good* idea. We should do that at the B and B!"

Lucy nodded. Having warm clothes and winter adventure gear *was* a pretty good idea and would make it a lot easier for guests to visit them during the winter from other, warmer places. No one wanted to buy a whole new winter wardrobe just for one trip. Maybe this Great Peach Experiment to the Icehotel would turn out to be a good research adventure after all!

"You can go inside the changing rooms just over there and change into your long undies. That should be all you need under your Icehotel snowsuit. Any more than undies, and you'll likely get a bit too warm," Josef told them. Freddy giggled. "You did bring long undies, correct? It was on the packing list we sent you!" Freddy giggled again, and Lucy suspected it was because Josef kept saying "undies."

Herb tugged at Lucy's arm and pulled her over to one side of the large equipment room. "I forgot," he said.

"Forgot what?" Lucy asked. "Your long undies?" Freddy, who was standing nearby, giggled again.

Herb nodded.

"But I saw them in your suitcase!" Lucy argued. "Right next to your flannel jammies and your clean undies and warm socks." Another Freddy giggle.

Herb gulped. "I took all that stuff out."

"Your clean underwear?" Lucy clarified.

"*All* my underwear," Herb said softly. "Long undies and clean undies and a bunch of other stuff, too."

Now Freddy was practically doubled over with laughter.

Nearby, Dad had stepped into a massive blue snowsuit and was parading around the equipment room looking very proud and warm. He was now about the same size and shape as Josef—round and smooshy and not at all like the tall, skinny dad he usually was. The giant suit seemed to gobble up whoever was inside and replace their former body with a giant, walking marshmallow.

"You took stuff out of your suitcase?" Lucy clarified. "After Dad and I checked it over to make sure you had everything you needed?"

Herb chewed his lip. "I took all my stuff out so I could fit my Beanie Babies collection in for the adventure. You know, the ones I got from Trudie at Birch Pond?" Herb had received a stuffed animal as a gift from Trudie every time he visited her at Great Aunt Lucinda's retirement

center. He'd built up quite the collection, and Herb had always been *very* attached to his collections and treasures. "But then I forgot to put all my clothes back *in* my suitcase, so now I think I only have Beanie Babies in my bag and no undies to wear at all!"

Freddy snorted. Lucy glared at him. "Fred, it's not funny. What if Herb has to go *naked* under his snowsuit?" This question made Freddy shriek with laughter and sent Herb into a fit of tears brought on from too little sleep. Lucy closed her eyes. "Don't worry, Herbie. You won't *actually* have to go naked, but I'm not sure what we're going to do about this. Do you have *any* clothes in your bag, or is it just filled with stuffies?"

"I can't remember," Herb sniffed. "I was so busy making sure all my friends and collections fit that I can't remember what I took out and what I left in."

"Maybe they have something you can borrow to wear under your snowsuit," Lucy suggested, hoping this was true. They seemed to have a lot of stuff for people to use.

"I'm not borrowing someone else's undies—long *or* regular," Herb announced, loudly enough that Josef, Dad, and Great Aunt Lucinda heard him. "I'd rather go naked under my suit."

"What's all this about?" Dad asked, swishing over in his giant suit. He'd added a huge fur-lined hat and a face cover to his ensemble. You could barely even see who was under all those warm layers.

"Herb unpacked most of his clothes and his long underwear," Freddy tattled. "So that he could fit all his stuffed animals into his suitcase."

Dad shook his head, and the fluffy fur of his hat waved as he turned this way and that. "I stuck your long underwear in my bag, bud," he told Herb. "I spotted them on the floor next to your suitcase before we left for the airport and was worried you were going to forget them."

"Oh," Herb said, smiling through his tears. "Thanks, Dad."

This version of Dad—the responsible, caring dad he'd become over the past few months—still sometimes felt strange and unfamiliar to Lucy. After their mom had died, Dad had fallen deep into his own grief and kind of forgot how to be a parent for a while. Lucy had taken on a lot of the jobs their parents used to do—keeping track of missing school assignments for her brothers, making dinner many nights, tucking Herb in and reading him a chapter of a book before bed, and other stuff that Dad couldn't remember. But ever since their big summer trip in the Peach Pie Truck, Dad had been working really hard to *be* there more.

Lucy loved that he was the kind of dad they could count on now. He was still a little scatterbrained and sometimes forgot things, but he always made Lucy and her brothers his priority lately, and that felt good. Dad's promises were real promises, not just things he said and then forgot about later.

Lucy dug her own long underwear out of her suitcase, and saw that Freddy was doing the same thing. "As soon as you're all ready," Josef said, "I can walk you around so you have a chance to explore the beautiful Icehotel tonight, then I think you will all want to have some food and climb into a warm bed to get some sleep?" He glanced over, catching Lucy mid-yawn. She was *tired*. Like, drop right here and sleep on the floor tired.

She looked to her right and noticed that Great Aunt Lucinda had fallen asleep on a bench at the edge of the room. Herb was swaying on his feet. Freddy was the only Peach who looked like he still had any energy left in him at all.

"Or . . ." Josef said, cringing when Great Aunt Lucinda's head dipped to her chest and her wig slid off her head. "We could save the Icehotel tour and equipment fitting for tomorrow and let you all get settled into your warm hotel room now? That way you can have something wonderful to look forward to when you wake up in the morning!"

"That might be best," Dad said, already peeling off his snowsuit and hat. "I think our crew is very tired."

"I'm not!" Freddy argued. "I want to see the Icehotel. I don't want to wait until morning—we've been stuck on planes forever, and I want to see the thing we came here for!"

Herb sat down next to Great Aunt Lucinda and lay his head in her lap. Lucy was very temped to join them, but she *was* excited to see the frozen hotel and all the ice carvings right away. Though there wasn't a huge rush, since they *did* have all week to explore everything. . . .

"How about this," Josef said, his round cheeks rosy. "I can take Mister Freddy, along with anyone else from your family who wants to come along, on a tour now. Those who would rather go to bed and save their tour of the Icehotel for morning can go to bed. We don't need to do everything as a group. There is a small meeting planned with some of the other sweepstakes winners tonight, so we can talk to you all about the Frozen Olympics we have planned, but we can always fill the rest of you in later. My job here is to make you comfortable and help you enjoy yourselves."

Ah, Lucy thought to herself. *So* that's *his job?* Was Josef the Peach family Icehotel butler? Would he be at their beck and call during the trip? Maybe they ought to provide butler services to their guests at the B&B!

"That seems fair," Dad agreed. "Why don't I take Great Aunt Lucinda and Herb to our room in the warm hotel for the night, and Lucy and Freddy can take some time to explore with you, Josef." He glanced at Lucy for approval. Much as she wanted to go to bed, she wanted to see the Icehotel *more*. And a meeting with all the other sweepstakes winners was not something she wanted to miss. She was glad Dad had offered to take the other two to their rooms, since both Great Aunt Lucinda and Herb were now fast asleep on the bench inside the toasty-warm equipment room.

Josef grinned. "Wonderful. Lucy and Freddy, if you'll just find suits that fit and finish getting all your warm gear on, I'll meet you right back here after I've shown the other Peaches to their rooms. Dad Peach, I'll also have some food sent up from the restaurant so you can go to sleep on a full stomach."

As soon as the others were gone, Lucy looked at her brother and they both started laughing. "He's going to have food sent up? Free winter gear to borrow? A personalized tour of the Icehotel? Ice-carving lessons?" Freddy said, obviously impressed. "Whoa, they take comfort and hospitality to a whole new level here."

Lucy nodded. She began digging through the racks of snowsuits, eventually pulling out a dark purple one that looked like it was about the right size. It had a fluffy white fake-fur collar around the hood and white racing stripes up the side. It was perfect. She stepped into it, then zipped it up and gave her brother a thumbs-up. "This is going to be the best vacation ever."

As soon as she said it, a voice rang out behind them. "Um, *excuse* me? That's *my* snowsuit."

Lucy spun around. There was a girl about her own age standing in the middle of the equipment room, glaring in her direction. "I'm so sorry," Lucy said quickly. "I thought these were all available. I just picked one that looked good, and—"

"And assumed you could just take it?" the girl snapped, in what was clearly American English. "You won a sweepstakes, so now you're entitled to anything and everything you see here?"

Lucy's mouth dropped open. "Um, I don't—"

"Well, you need to pick a new one, because this one's already taken." As soon as Lucy had stepped out of the snowsuit, the girl swiped it out of Lucy's hands. Then she stormed toward the changing room, calling back over her shoulder, "And for your information, The Under the Sea Suite in the Icehotel is already claimed for tomorrow night. By me and my family. Figured I should tell you now before you try to take that, too."

The door to the changing room slammed behind her and the girl was gone.

Lucy and Freddy exchanged a look. As her brother began to laugh again, Lucy shrugged and said, "Okay, then . . . I guess I better pick a new snowsuit."

From the Sketchbook of Freddy Peach:

ICEHOTEL STAFF

Josef

Philip

4

From the Sketchbook of Freddy Noodle:

ICEHOTEL STAFF

ICY EXPLORATIONS

Stepping out of the warm equipment room into the frosty evening air was both alarming and thrilling. It felt like it was close to 100 degrees colder *outside* than *in*, and even wrapped up in his snazzy new green-and-yellow Icehotel snowsuit, Freddy could tell exactly how cold the air was because his eyeballs felt like they were close to icing over as soon as he got outside. Frozen eyeballs were something he'd felt in Minnesota, but never quite like this, and never so late in winter when warm spring weather was so close around the corner.

Freddy sometimes wondered if eyeballs could *actually* ice over, or if it just felt like they were freezing when it was super cold out. Eyes were wet, so when frozen air hit them, shouldn't they ice up the way a wet car windshield would? Snotty nose hairs froze all the time.

Damp head hair froze whenever he came out of the Y after his winter swimming lessons. His eyelashes sometimes iced up and froze into clumps when he was playing in the snow in the backyard. Why didn't his eyeballs freeze into place when they were in subzero temperatures? This was a question he decided he would need to explore further.

But for the moment, Freddy had to focus all his attention on walking behind Josef without falling over. The Icehotel snowsuits were big, bulky, and made him and Lucy look like snow beasts. They'd hustled to grab their borrowed winter gear and had just thrown their suits and boots and hats and mittens on over their regular clothes, since Lucy hadn't wanted to risk bumping into the unfriendly girl in the women's changing area. So now, they were both extra bulky and very warm as they followed their new friend Josef down a snow-packed path that led from the equipment room to the Icehotel's frozen centerpiece building.

As they waddled across the hotel property's grounds, a dogsledding team ran past on the snow-covered street—right where Josef had driven them in with the van that afternoon. Nearby, a person (under all those clothes, it was hard to tell if it was a woman or man, child or adult) stood under a giant spotlight carving a mermaid out of a block of ice. Before he could get a good look at the sculpture, Lucy grabbed Freddy's arm and tugged him in the other direction. She pointed; there was a pair of what looked like *reindeer*, just hanging out in someone's giant, snowy yard!

Little twinkle lights hung from some of the trees overhead, and ice-carved lanterns lined the road and walkways, making the whole atmosphere around the Icehotel feel like a winter wonderland Freddy had only seen before in paintings and on TV.

The lingering afternoon light had quickly faded to darkness while they were inside the equipment room, and now the inky sky was frosted with a sprinkling of stars. Up ahead of them, the frozen Icehotel appeared to glow under blue and white and pink lights. The structure's entrance was illuminated with a bright yellow spotlight that called attention to the antlers that served as the handles on the hotel's grand front doors. "Here we are at the world-famous, frozen Icehotel!" Josef said loudly, stating the obvious. "We can spend a few minutes taking a quick tour inside, and then we'll need to meet the other sweepstakes winners in the Ice Bar to talk about your stay and some of the things we have planned for you with the Frozen Olympics."

"Ice Bar?" Freddy asked. But Josef didn't answer.

Freddy suspected he must not have heard the question, since it was a little tough to hear much through all the layers of warm fabric and fur.

Inside, the Icehotel was much more magnificent than Freddy could have ever imagined. And miraculously, it was much warmer in here than it was outside! A giant crystal chandelier—no, this was made of ice, too!—hung overhead, and all the walls were made of blocks of frozen river water that had been carved into patterns and shapes and glimmering artwork. The reflection of lights inside the building made everything glow, and the walls sparkled and almost seemed as if they'd come to life around them. "It looks like a crystal palace," Lucy said, looping her arm through Freddy's as they followed Josef down a long, wide, icy hallway.

As they walked, they passed other people wearing snowsuits that were like Freddy's and Lucy's, but in a rainbow of different colors that created a stark contrast against the icy white walls. Freddy suddenly realized all the people kind of looked like a bunch of colorful Lucky Charms cereal marshmallows, floating in a sea of pure milk. Freddy's stomach rumbled, reminding him that they hadn't eaten since the snack they'd had on the plane ride from Stockholm to Kiruna. But for once in his life, Freddy was more excited about a tour than he was about food. He could eat later; his first glimpse of a building made entirely of ice was happening *now.*

"This is the Great Hall," Josef said, stopping in the middle of a large room with carvings of faces in the ice blocks that lined the walls. "This year, the hotel's chief designer took inspiration from many different medieval castles and the art and people who lived in them when thinking about how to design our shared space in the hotel. The designer is Scottish, and castles are a big part of her cultural heritage."

Freddy nodded appreciatively. When he'd designed his dream treehouse for an art competition a few months back, he'd gotten inspiration for each of the rooms in the treehouse he built from the things and activities his family loved most. He knew that most—possibly all—great artists found inspiration for their art from something important in their own lives. Freddy hoped he'd be inspired to create some new art after this trip. But more than anything he hoped his family would be inspired to find ways to attract guests to The Peachtree B&B. They *really* needed more customers to start booking rooms, and Freddy hoped they could figure out how to make that happen before their string of good luck began to run out. Because he knew it probably *would* run out . . . eventually.

Yet this good luck streak of theirs had lasted a while now—first, Mom's invention had sold and made them millionaires; next, they'd earned the grand prize at the Ohio Food Truck Festival; then, Great Aunt Lucinda had given them a house *and* they'd done all the work they needed to do to keep it; and now, they'd won a huge sweepstakes to take a fancy, once-in-a-lifetime trip. Each of their Great Peach Experiments had ended in their favor . . . up to now. How many more things could possibly go right before everything began to swing back the other way again? They'd had several years of very, very *bad* luck before things had gotten better, so Freddy knew all too well not to assume there would always be a happy ending to every adventure.

After passing an enormous ice dragon, and several thrones made of ice that looked like glass and had been stained to look like jewels, Josef led Lucy and Freddy out the other end of the Great Hall. They followed him down a tight hallway that was glowing bright orange from lanterns that looked like torches (but couldn't possibly *be* torches, since fire plus ice would not end well). "Next," Josef said, his voice muffled by his snowsuit. "We'll be visiting some of the unique Ice Suites in the hotel. Each one is designed by a different artist; we invite the designers here from around the world. They each choose a theme that speaks to them and design a room that showcases their artistic style—using only ice."

The first room seemed to have an outer space theme—the bed, which was a massive slab of ice covered in a giant fur, looked like a rocket ship and was lit from within. The whole room had a sort of red glow to it, making Freddy think of Mars. "You'll have more time to explore all the rooms for much longer on your own time tomorrow; tonight, I just want to give you a quick preview of all the Icehotel has to offer, and then I'll bring you to the meeting with the other sweepstakes winners."

Freddy could have wandered through each of the Ice Suites for hours, carefully studying each of the room designs. He'd never seen anything like this. Every once in a while, he remembered he was standing under thousands of pounds—*tons*—of ice that could collapse or melt at any moment. But mostly, he was distracted by all the little details in each room, and how each artist had managed to use the same ingredients—ice, carving tools, and watercolor or food coloring—to create such different masterpieces. Just like a painter used brushes, a blank canvas, and paint; or how a sculptor used clay, tools, and water to create their art. The one thing they all had in common was an imagination and a wish to create something new where there'd been just blah raw materials before.

When they got to a room labeled UNDER THE SEA, Freddy nudged Lucy. "Hey, check it out—this is your friend's room."

Lucy rolled her eyes at him. "*Not* my friend."

Freddy looked all around The Under the Sea Suite but couldn't find any stuff that suggested this room had already been claimed or that someone would be sleeping here anytime soon. "Where are all the guests' suitcases?" he asked Josef.

"Ah, yes, that is a good question," Josef said with a smile. "People leave their things in one of the warm rooms that are connected to the Icehotel—they're a bit like locker rooms, with warm bathrooms and running water for drinking. We only use the Ice Suites for sleeping and relaxing at night, but during the day you'll always have a heated space to keep your things and get a break from the cold if you need it." He led them back out into the icy hallway, past more suites that they didn't get to peek inside. "Tomorrow, your family will have a chance to admire all the frozen rooms together, and then you can choose which one you'd like to sleep in during your night on ice."

"We only get to sleep one night inside the Icehotel?"

Freddy asked. "What about all the other nights we're here?"

"Most of our guests choose to spend only one night in the Ice Suites, just to say they did it," Josef told them as they strolled through the Great Hall together. "All the other nights they're visiting us, most people choose to sleep in our warm hotel on the other side of the property that is *not* made of ice."

"What if I say I want to spend *more* than one night on ice?" Freddy asked. He hadn't come all this way to sleep in a regular old hotel! He lived in a hotel at home; here in Sweden, he wanted the full Icehotel experience.

Josef laughed. "If that's your wish, we can make it happen. You can choose a different suite to sleep in each night, if you so choose, and decide for yourself which one is most comfortable."

"Are you serious?" Freddy asked. Lucy was looking at him warily. "I can switch rooms every night, and spend the whole week living inside different rooms in a giant ice castle?"

"As long as your dad is okay with it, it's fine with the Icehotel." Josef gestured for them to follow him into another icy room on the far end of the Great Hall. "Now, come—it's time to meet some of the other sweepstakes winners and learn all about the activities available to you during your week in the Arctic. Of course, we have other guests staying at the Icehotel now as well, but we have many special things planned just for all of you who are here as our prize-winning guests."

Lucy nudged Freddy—hard enough that he could feel it through all the warm layers—in the side. "You can't be serious?" she asked. "You want to sleep inside a frozen room every night we're here?"

"Of course," Freddy said. "Who *wouldn't*?"

"Me, for one," Lucy said. "And anyone else who's warm-blooded. It's *cold* in here. It will be like sleeping in a walk-in freezer for a week straight!"

Freddy patted his hands on his puffy chest. "Ah, but I have a cozy snowsuit to keep me warm. Come on, Luce, join me. It will be fun."

Lucy laughed. "I'll let you be the *cool* guy who freezes to death, Fred. After my single night sleeping on a block of ice tomorrow night, I'm going to snuggle up in a warm bed in the regular hotel and enjoy the cold during the day only, thank y—"

Freddy grabbed his sister's arm, cutting her off. Using his eyes, he gestured across the room to a group of about a dozen people sitting in clusters around booths, stools, and tables, all of which were made of ice.

Everyone was sipping drinks through paper straws in frozen goblets (even the glasses appeared to be made from chunks of ice!). Right in the center of the group was the girl who'd yelled at Lucy for stealing her snowsuit.

"Ugh," Lucy grumbled quietly to Freddy. "Is she one of the sweepstakes winners?"

As if in answer to Lucy's question, Josef led them straight to the group gathered on the far side of the Ice Bar. "And here we are! Everyone, meet Lucy and Freddy Peach. Peaches, these are some of the other lucky families who have won the Icehotel sweepstakes."

Several people waved and others smiled. But the girl in the purple snowsuit did neither. She just looked at them, her face expressionless and cold.

"Hi, everyone!" Freddy said loudly. During their time running the Peach Pie Truck, Freddy had found that friendliness was usually met with friendliness, so he always tried to win people over by being extra nice . . . especially when it seemed like they were having a bad day. And Snowsuit Girl definitely seemed to be having a not-great day. "I'm Freddy Peach, and this is my older sister, Lucy. We're from Duluth, Minnesota, and we run The Peachtree B and B."

"Hi, there," an older gentleman called out from

the farthest table over. He was sitting with a woman around his own age, a younger man, and a boy who was around six or seven. "We're the Banerjees, and we own Anderson's Resort in the Upper Peninsula of Michigan."

Freddy was just puzzling out why the *Banerjee* family would name their resort after someone else's last name when the younger guy said, "We bought the place from Harold Anderson and didn't want to change the name and lose long-standing guests who might get confused."

"Gotcha," Freddy said, nodding. "That makes sense."

A couple of guys who were a little younger than Dad introduced themselves and their twin daughters—who looked to be a little younger than Herb—as the Weiss-Buckthorn family, and said they ran a little seaside bed-and-breakfast in northern Washington State.

A woman and her mom—who were probably about Dad and Great Aunt Lucinda's age—stood up and announced that they were the mother-daughter duo of Janice and Janeen Murphy, and they owned a group of cottages "in the middle of nowhere, way up in Maine." Freddy wasn't sure which one of them was Janice and which was Janeen, and to be totally honest, he wasn't entirely sure which was the mom and which was the daughter. They looked almost exactly alike inside their giant snowsuits.

The last group of people to introduce themselves was the family with Lucy's new best friend. The girl in the purple snowsuit who they'd already met stood up and said, "I'm Ellen Proetz, and this is my amazing family—" She gestured to a boy who looked like he was probably older, and another who was somewhere around Herb's age, as well as a woman and a man who Freddy guessed were her parents. "We own and operate the award-winning Proetz Family Farm in the mountains of Montana. Which we built ourselves, with wood harvested by hand from the property."

Freddy nodded approvingly. The girl had confidence, there was no denying that, and it sounded like her family knew how to run a successful business. And they had built a whole *hotel* with their own hands? Maybe he and Lucy could win Ellen over and get some tips from her.

"I'm glad you all took a few minutes to introduce yourselves," Josef said, stepping forward along with several other Icehotel staff members. Freddy knew they must be staff, since they were all wearing matching yellow snowsuits with their names sewn onto a patch on the front of the suits. "We're missing a few of the Peach family sweep-stakes winners who just arrived in Sweden this afternoon and have retired to their rooms for the night."

Lucy leaned toward Freddy and said, "Did some of the people get here earlier than us?"

Freddy shrugged, but he guessed Lucy couldn't see it through his snowsuit. "Dunno," he said aloud. "Any guesses where we can get one of those drinks in the ice cups?"

As soon as he said it, a woman holding a tray of bev-erages came parading by. She offered one to both Freddy and Lucy, explaining, "It's lingonberry juice. Drink it quick, or it will freeze to the inside of your cup."

Freddy did as he was told, glugging down the delicious juice while Josef and his cowork-ers introduced themselves. It still wasn't clear what anyone's job was, but it *was* clear that the Peaches would have more than enough things to do during their trip. They could choose any activities that interested them: dogsledding lessons, ice-carving demonstrations and practice, cooking classes in the warm hotel, sledding and tobogganing, cross-country skiing and snowshoeing, spa treatments, snowmobile expeditions, and some other things Freddy didn't pay much attention to, since he didn't think they sounded interesting at all.

"But the best thing we have planned for you sweepstakes winners this week," a tall, smiley guy named Anders said, "is our very special Frozen Olympics."

Freddy rubbed his hands together. *This* was what he'd been waiting for. His family thrived when they were given a goal, and he knew they had what it would take to win this Frozen Olympics.

Anders continued. "As you can see, our five sweepstakes-winning families all hail from chilly places in America—Maine, Washington, Montana, Michigan, and Minnesota. When we saw where our winners all lived, we thought it would be fun to give each of your families a chance to compete up here in the Arctic, to see which of you can take home the title of Frozen Best."

Freddy whooped aloud. Lucy jabbed him with an elbow and Freddy nearly dropped his empty ice mug.

"Starting tomorrow, we'll be hosting a collection of different competitions up here in our frozen wonderland, and we'll keep a running tally of points you all win during the week. We're going to have an ice-carving contest, sledding races, a snowperson-building contest, a cooking competition, and the grand finale: a dogsledding adventure race, in a sled your family will have a chance to decorate together, that will be held on your last full day here." Anders grinned. "So . . . who's in it to win it?"

"What will we win?" meanie-Ellen blurted out from the front.

"The *winner*," Anders said, winking at her, "which might be you, or might *not* be you, will receive . . . a custom Ice Castle, built by one of our artists at your very own hotel, lodge, or bed-and-breakfast next winter. This will be a special opportunity to have a little of the Icehotel experience at *your* place in America, which will hopefully help you attract even more customers to your inn."

"Our farm is already full all winter," Ellen scoffed. "We don't need more business." Her dad looked embarrassed by Ellen's announcement but nodded as if to say that she was telling the truth. Freddy normally didn't like to judge people too quickly . . . but based on the first few encounters he'd had with Ellen, he had the feeling she wasn't going to be his favorite person on earth.

"Then you can choose not to participate in the Frozen Olympics," Anders told her. "Or compete just for fun. But our hope is that this will be something exciting for all of you to take part in this week, and the sugar on top is that one of your families—our Frozen Best—will get to take home yet another special prize at the end of it. Sound good?"

Freddy clapped his big leather mittens together—and was surprised at how loud it was. Soon, all the other sweepstakes winners began to talk among themselves about the Frozen Olympics. Freddy couldn't wait to tell Dad, Herb, and Great Aunt Lucinda everything they'd learned, first thing in the morning when the rest of the family woke up. "We're gonna win," Freddy whispered to Lucy as they followed Josef back through the Icehotel to the warm hotel and their waiting dinner.

"We need to beat that girl Ellen, that's for sure," Lucy agreed.

Freddy wasn't all that concerned with who they did or didn't beat. He just wanted to make sure they *won*. He wanted that prize. The Peaches *needed* the prize so they could have an ice castle of their very own in Duluth. But he also wanted to win so he'd know that their good luck hadn't yet run out. Because the alternative frightened him; the last thing they needed was another string of bad luck. "Peaches: Frozen Best," Freddy said, nodding. "I like the ring of that."

FREDDY'S HANDY-DANDY FROZEN OLYMPICS COMPETITOR GUIDE

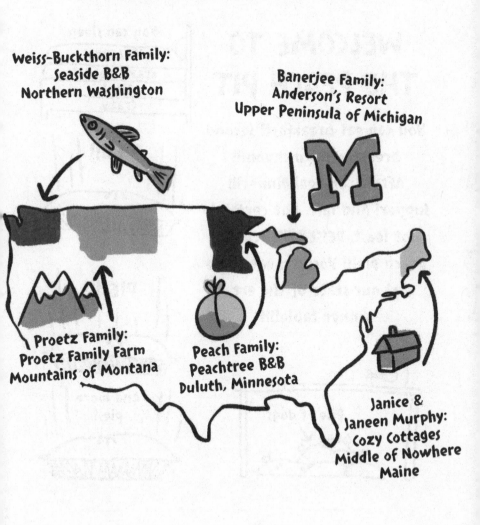

Weiss-Buckthorn Family:
Seaside B&B
Northern Washington

Banerjee Family:
Anderson's Resort
Upper Peninsula of Michigan

Proetz Family:
Proetz Family Farm
Mountains of Montana

Peach Family:
Peachtree B&B
Duluth, Minnesota

Janice &
Janeen Murphy:
Cozy Cottages
Middle of Nowhere
Maine

From the Sketchbook of Freddy Peach:

B&B ADVERTISING IDEAS

WELCOME TO THE PEACH PIT

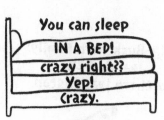

You can sleep IN A BED! crazy right?? Yep! Crazy.

You can eat breakfast! Second breakfast!! Luncheon!!! Afternoon tea! Dinner!!! Supper! And last, but certainly not least, DESSERT!!! Try our peach pie!!! You can eat those at our state of the art dinner table!!!!

PIES!!!

PIES!!!

And more pies!

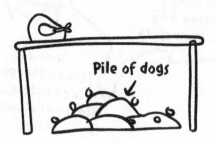

Pile of dogs

5

TOURING THE ICE SUITES

Lucy woke up the next morning to find Herb bouncing on the edge of her cozy bed in their warm hotel room, wearing Great Aunt Lucinda's long, lavender Purple Rain wig. "Morning, Lucy," he said, hugging her tight. Strands of the straight, wiry wig hair tickled her cheeks, and several found their way into her open, yawning mouth.

"*Mrmph*," Lucy replied, covering her face with the fluffy pillow from the other side of her very own double bed. She and Great Aunt Lucinda were sharing one room, and Dad had decided to bunk with the boys. Lucy knew all too well that she had won the lottery with this room assignment. Unlike Dad, Great Aunt Lucinda did not snore and she kept a bag of fancy chocolates in a quilted bag on the table between their beds—that Lucy had been invited to dig into anytime, day or night. "What time is it?"

"Six thirty in the morning," Herb declared proudly. "We slept for almost twelve hours!"

"*You* slept for almost twelve hours," Lucy told him. "Freddy and I didn't get to bed until after nine last night." She was exhausted from jet lag, but Lucy was glad Herb had woken her up. There was so much to do up here on the Icehotel grounds, and Lucy didn't want to waste any of her time sleeping in. Suddenly, her stomach rumbled, reminding Lucy that all she'd had for dinner the night before had been a cold ham sandwich. She was starving.

As she pulled on clothes, Lucy noticed that Great Aunt Lucinda was already up and out of their shared room. That would explain how Herb had snuck his head into one of her wigs; Great Aunt Lucinda took care of her fake hair the way some people cared for their pets, and Lucy had a feeling she wouldn't like knowing Herb was trying out one of her looks when she wasn't around to stop him.

Fortunately, Herb carefully tucked Great Aunt Lucinda's wig back into its nest in the drawer where she'd unpacked it for the week, and then led Lucy down to the small dining room on the bottom floor of the warm hotel. "Warm hotel" is what she and Freddy had decided to call the ordinary, regular hotel where most of the family would sleep most nights during their vacation. The warm hotel was small and comfortable, and the rooms were full of pretty art and wood walls, but it was nothing super-special. Lucy was definitely looking forward to her upcoming night of sleeping on ice in order to get the full Icehotel experience, but she had a feeling she'd be equally excited to return to her plush, comfy, not-frozen bed for the rest of the trip.

Great Aunt Lucinda, Dad, and Freddy were all sitting together at a table covered in plates filled with hearty slices of bread and a variety of cheeses, a little basket filled with hard-boiled eggs, and a collection of tubes that looked like toothpaste. Lucy took a seat and studied one of the tubes.

"It's caviar," Freddy announced through a mouthful of bread and cheese. "That's fish eggs."

"I know what caviar is," Lucy told him. "But why is it at our table?"

"I guess it's part of the breakfast here," Freddy said with a shrug. "I tried it, because why not? It's crunchy and salty and awful." Lucy set the tube back down on the table. "I don't think we should add tubes

of caviar to our breakfast offerings at The Peachtree B and B."

"Good morning, Lucy," Dad said, pouring himself a fresh cup of coffee from the pot in the center of the table. "How did you sleep?"

"Really well," Lucy said, accepting the glass of pink juice a waiter offered her. She dug a boiled egg out of the basket, noticing that they were still warm.

"I hope I didn't wake you when I got dressed and put on my face," Great Aunt Lucinda said. "I couldn't sleep past five. Jet lag is a strange thing."

"Now that Lucy's here," Freddy said, grabbing a bowl of jam and digging his spoon into it. "We have so many things to tell you that we learned last night."

For the next ten minutes, Lucy and Freddy took turns sharing information about the Frozen Olympics, their option to sleep in an Ice Suite *every* night or just once (everyone except Freddy thought one night in a freezing cold room would be sufficient), the activity choices, and they also briefly told them about some of the other families who had won the sweepstakes and would be spending the week with them.

"How fun is it that everyone else who won is from other cold places," Dad said.

"The other winning families all seem pretty nice," Freddy said.

Lucy added, "Except one person." Then she used a snooty-sounding voice to say, "Ellen Proetz, of the Proetz Family Farm in Montana."

Dad gave her a stern look. "That's not a kind voice, Lulu."

"She's not a kind girl," Lucy said, but then immediately felt bad. Sure, Ellen hadn't been overly friendly—in fact, she'd been outright mean about the snowsuit and hastily calling dibs on one of the Ice Suites—but Lucy kept trying to remember that she didn't know the whole story. Maybe Ellen had a reason for why she'd been crabby when they'd bumped into her in the equipment room. Maybe she was a perfectly lovely person. Maybe she would become a lifelong friend and Lucy would get to visit their farm in Montana and Ellen could come visit The Peachtree B&B.

Or maybe . . . she really *was* icky, and Lucy's family would need to beat her in the Frozen Olympics to prove to her that the Peaches were amazing, too. "But I was tired when I met her," Lucy said, trying to set a good example for her brothers. "So maybe I read her wrong and she's not as bad as she seemed."

While they ate, more and more guests filtered into the hotel's restaurant. Lucy noticed the mother-daughter pair—the ones who ran a group of cottages in Maine, she thought she remembered—and the two men with the twin girls who owned a seaside B&B in Washington. She didn't see the Proetz family of Montana, or the Banerjees (the family who owned Anderson's Resort in Michigan).

The hotel's restaurant space was sort of dark, which made it feel cozy, and there were paintings and photographs hung all over the walls of icy-blue glaciers, beautiful waterfalls, previous seasons of the Icehotel designs, a lovely red-and-green church in the middle of a snowy wonderland, dogs, moose, and people all dressed up in the Icehotel's signature snowsuits.

After breakfast, the Peaches headed toward the equipment room to get suited up in their warm winter gear so they could head out into the cold and snow. Great Aunt Lucinda had already signed up for a day's worth of spa treatments and sauna visits, but she planned to join the rest of the family while they wandered around the inside of the Icehotel to explore, and was also going to join them for that afternoon's Frozen Olympics snow-person-building contest. "I'm not sleeping on any ice beds, mind you," she said. "I like my warm blankets and a toilet I can get to in the night without stepping on snow—but I am excited to walk around to have a little look-see."

Because Great Aunt Lucinda was planning to sleep every night of the stay in a warm hotel room, that meant the other Peaches could fit into any one of the Ice Suites that fit a family of four. Most of the time, Lucy didn't much like being a family of four. Everything had felt more *right* when Mom was still alive and their family was bigger. She'd trade *anything* to go back to how things were before they went from five to four. But Lucy, Herb, Freddy, and their dad had finally started to get used to their new normal as a family, and there were even a few times when being a four-pack helped make things easier. Most restaurant tables and hotel rooms were designed to fit four. Now that Lucy was old enough to ride up front, no one ever had to sit in the middle of the back seat when they were all riding in the car together. And here in Sweden, all four Peaches could spend a night sleeping on ice together.

As soon as they were all bundled up in their long underwear, snowsuits, boots, hats, and mittens, the

Peaches headed outside. Daylight was creeping up the horizon to shove out the darkness of the long Arctic night, and Lucy realized everything looked and felt much different than it had the evening before. It wasn't quite as magical without the twinkling lights and stars overhead, but it also felt warmer with the promise of sunshine ahead. Freddy had informed them all that the days were short and nights were long during the winter above the Arctic Circle, and Lucy was glad they weren't visiting the Icehotel in the middle of winter, when it was dark almost all day long!

When they passed the reindeer roaming around in the outdoor pen, Herb shrieked with joy. And when Josef skidded to a stop next to them, standing on the back of a sled being pulled by a team of six dogs all harnessed together—a mix of different-colored huskies, some with long, fluffy hair and others that were shorter-haired and sleek—he jumped with joy. "It's like we're staying in a real-life North Pole!" Herb cried out, rubbing each of the dogs on their heads as they panted, barked, and wriggled with energy. "I keep waiting for Santa Claus to come wandering by."

"No Santa Claus," Josef said with a laugh. "But there is a guy named Philip who works with me who looks a lot like him. Same beard and build."

"I want to meet Philip," Herb declared.

"Come on by the kennel later, and you can meet Philip and the dogs," Josef offered. "We can get you started with your first dogsledding lesson."

Lucy thought her brother might explode with delight. A day where he got to talk to a man who looked like a real-life Santa *and* have a meet-and-greet with a bunch of sled dogs? This was Herb's dream come true.

"I'll be there," Herb promised. "I can't wait!" Josef and his team zipped away, the dogs going silent and focused as soon as they got to run again.

Lucy was glad she and Freddy had gotten a chance to explore the Icehotel with Josef the night before, so they could act as tour guides for the rest of their family once they got inside the frozen building. It was also fun to get to watch someone else's reaction when they experienced the incredible and massive ice castle for the first time.

"Well, isn't that something . . ." Aunt Lucinda said, her eyes wide as she took in the massive Great Hall.

"I can't believe this whole thing melts each spring," Dad noted. "And then they build it all again the next year?"

Herb tugged Lucy's hand, dragging her toward the sleeping section of the hotel. "I want to pick our family's room for tonight," he declared. The Peaches headed down the frozen hall toward the one-of-a-kind Ice Suites to try to figure out which one they would choose to sleep in as a group that night. This morning, without Josef leading them around, the Peaches had plenty of time to explore all the details of each of the rooms.

Since their family had just gone through the process of decorating the three guest suites in The Peachtree B&B, Lucy understood how much thought must have gone into all of these rooms that were also amazing works of art. From the designs carved into the walls, to the shape and height of the beds, to the lighting choices that had been made to showcase the artists' carving creations.

Herb's favorite room was, obviously, the one filled with carved-ice animals. There was a pile of puppies carved into one corner of the room, icy kittens strutted across the headboard of one of the beds (which were both shaped like giant, icy dog beds), three pigs wrestled in a corner, and a giant frozen deer with a full set of antlers stood proudly in the center of everything like a room protector.

Freddy's favorite was, unsurprisingly, the outer space room they'd seen the night before. Lucy's middle brother was always drawn to the most unusual and unique parts of everything he came across.

Dad loved The Science Suite, which was set up to look like a lab—but made entirely of ice. This one used a lot of different colored lights to highlight all the tiny details and icy specimens on the lab tables that lined the walls of the room.

Great Aunt Lucinda said if *she* were going to spend the night inside an ice room, she'd obviously choose The Queen's Suite, which looked exactly like a royal room in a castle. This suite looked like it fit best with the hotel's Great Hall and overall style of that year's Icehotel, since it sort of followed the same theme. And the fun thing about The Queen's Suite was, the beds were shaped like two giant thrones!

As luck would have it, Lucy's favorite room was, unfortunately, The Under the Sea Suite. She wasn't sure if she would have liked this one as much if she hadn't known Ellen's family had already called dibs on it, but that piece of information made her want to sleep under the frozen sea more than anywhere else. Maybe Lucy could convince her own family to wait a few nights to spend their night on ice, and they could take a turn after Ellen's family was done using it? If each family spent

only one night sleeping inside the cold rooms of the Icehotel, that could work . . . right?

After they'd filled nearly an hour exploring all the
nooks and crannies of the Icehotel, the Peaches headed
back outside to have a look around the grounds. Their
giant snowsuits kept them warm and toasty, but Lucy
couldn't help but wonder how long they would be able to
hang out in the frozen air.

"Would you kids mind if I peel off for a bit to stop
by and say hello to the researchers I've been emailing
with up here?" Dad asked. He pointed down the road
and added, "Their office is just down thataway, and I'd
love to swing by and find out when they're planning to
head up to the research station this week. I don't want
to miss my chance to see what kinds of things they've
been working on!"

"That's fine," Lucy said. "I'll take Herb over to
the kennels and we can visit the sled dogs. Maybe we
can just meet you at the snowperson-building contest
later?"

Dad nodded, smiling gratefully at Lucy. "Let's all
plan to meet at the first Frozen Olympics competition
this afternoon," Dad said. "That's a great idea."

"Then I'm gonna explore some more and find out
where they do the ice-carving lessons," Freddy said.

"Unless Fred needs me to stick with him, I'll go in and get set for my spa treatments," Great Aunt Lucinda said with a wink. "And maybe take a little nap in that cozy bed."

Freddy nodded. "I'm fine on my own. If I get lost, I can just look for the giant building made of ice and find my way back."

Dad groaned. "Freddy, do *not* wander off the Ice-hotel grounds. Do I have your word on that?"

"Aye, aye, Captain!" Freddy said with a smile and a salute.

Dad went one way, Freddy another, and Great Aunt Lucinda headed toward the warm hotel. Meanwhile, Lucy led her youngest brother back down the road toward the kennel building she and Freddy had passed the night before. Even if she hadn't known where it was, the sounds of barking would have clued anyone in to the dogsledding kennel's whereabouts.

"Hello?" Lucy called out, popping the front door of the big, red, wooden building open a crack.

"Come on in," a voice called back. "I'm getting the dogs' food ready!"

From the street, the kennel looked like it was way too small to house dozens of dogs. But when they went through the front door, Lucy and Herb found it was a giant, open-plan building that felt a lot like a big barn.

There were only a few dogs roaming around the barn (including a litter of puppies in an enclosed area that had a flap that allowed them to move between the inside of the barn and the snowy outside yard at will) and a man who looked exactly like Santa Claus in a flannel shirt and jeans. "Hey, hey," the guy said. *"Valkommen."*

"Tack so mycket," Herb said, and again, Lucy marveled at the fact that her eight-year-old brother had taken it upon himself to learn some Swedish before their trip.

"Ah, pratar tu Svenska?" the Santa-man said with a huge smile. His big, rosy cheeks looked like two apples on either side of his face when he smiled.

"Sorry, no. I only speak a *little* bit of Swedish," Herb said apologetically. "But I'm learning."

"Very nice," the man told him. He was mixing up a slurry of dog mush inside a giant bucket. "I'm Philip. And you are?"

"My name is Herb Peach," Herb declared. "And this is my big sister, Lucy. Josef told us we could come by and meet the dogs."

"We can come back later," Lucy said hurriedly. "If now's a bad time."

"Never a bad time," Philip said. "I'm always happy to have some help feeding the pack, and then if you like, you can help me get some of the dogs harnessed up for their afternoon runs."

Herb's eyes went as wide as two full moons. "Okay!"

Philip led them out into the huge, tree-lined yard behind the kennel building. Dozens of dogs—maybe even a hundred of them!—were curled up or standing in the snow on what looked to be *acres* of fenced-in land. Each dog was tethered to a metal stake by a chain, and each pup had its very own elevated doghouse right in the center of its little circle. When the dogs spotted their human guests, they all began barking, jumping for attention, or playing and wrestling with a friend-dog in a neighboring circle. "Whoa," Lucy said loudly, hoping to be heard over the frenzied dog-chatting. "That's a lot of dogs."

"This is just half the crew out here now; the rest of them are gone on runs," Philip said, dragging the giant dog food bucket outside.

"What's in there?" Herb asked, gesturing to the disgusting, sloppy mixture.

"It's a mix of kibble, ground-up meat, and some water to keep them hydrated," Philip said.

As soon as Philip filled each of the dogs' bowls—most of which were attached to the side of their individual houses—the pup dug in, eagerly gobbling up its meal. Though some dogs were huge and others quite a bit smaller, each of these dogs were all at least four times the size of Dasher, Donner, Vix, and Rudy—the Peaches' dogs back at home. Though they looked nothing like the Peaches' naughty little pups, Lucy suddenly really missed their pack as she and Herb trailed after Philip through the yard. Even if they were *very* mischievous and badly behaved pretty much all of the time, the four little dogs had really grown on Lucy.

Philip told them each dog's name as he doled out food, and a few fun facts about each. "You'll meet the others later, when they return from their morning trips."

"Do the dogs spend all day out here when they're not off on an adventure?" Lucy asked. "Don't they get cold?"

"Nah," Philip said, giving a few of the dogs a vigorous ear rub as he finished his feeding rounds. "They like being outside. They grow an extra layer of fur in the winter, so they'd be miserable in a heated house. They'd all *rather* be out running, but when they're here at home, they love hanging out in the yard in their circles."

"Are those the sleds?" Herb asked, pointing to a corner of the yard Lucy hadn't noticed because she'd been too busy watching and petting all the dogs. Under a large, covered area, there were dozens of sleds lined up, side by side, just waiting for someone to hop on and take a ride. Some were narrow and sleek, others wider, and a few looked like small boats.

"Yes, sir," Philip said, leading them over to the sled storage area. "These are the sleds you'll be riding, if you decide you want to learn to mush during your visit to the Icehotel. As a matter of fact, since you're here, now would be a good time for you to choose a sled for your family for the final event in the Frozen Olympics. You'll have a chance to spend some time this week decorating it a bit. Of course, the fastest dogsled team will win the final event in the Frozen Olympics, but we'll be giving out a bonus point to whichever sled design most impresses the judges."

Lucy grinned. This was great! Ellen and her family may have gotten first dibs on their Ice Suite to sleep in, but she and Herb got to pick the Peach family *sled* first. This would definitely give them an advantage in the final race! Herb immediately started investigating all the sleds, trying to figure out which one looked like a winner. But Lucy realized the best way to choose would be to leave it up to the expert. "Which one would *you* choose, if you were going to race in one?" she asked Philip.

"Hmmm," he said, scanning the selection of sleds. "Sort of depends."

"On what?" Lucy asked.

"Well, how many people are going to be riding with you," Philip said. "And if you're more interested in speed, or stability."

"Speed," Herb said, at the same time as Lucy said, "Stability."

Philip laughed. "I actually think Lucy might have the right idea here," he told them. "A fast sled isn't going to do you any good if it tips or you can't control it. And since you only have a few days to learn to mush, I'm guessing you're not going to get to be true experts before the big race. So, keeping your sled under control is probably going to give you the biggest advantage in the race."

Lucy grinned. Then she asked, "How many people *can* fit on a sled?"

"You could comfortably get three people in, but any more than that and weight is going to be a factor," Philip said. "That's something to consider when you're figuring out how to decorate your sled, as well. You won't want to use anything too heavy or elaborate, since the dogs will need to pull it all."

"Just three?" Herb said, sounding disappointed. "But there are five members of our family."

Lucy assured Herb that they'd be able to figure out a great team of three to race their family's sled by the end of the week. She'd be willing to sit it out and cheer if she had to. They didn't all have to do everything together!

"I'd go with this one," Philip said, pointing to a sled with a comfortable-looking compartment that looked like it would just *barely* fit two people riding inside. "If you want to claim it as yours for the big race, I'll set it aside in your area, and then you can swing by and work on decorating it whenever you have some free time this week."

Lucy couldn't wait to tell Freddy about this little bonus part of the Frozen Olympics. As an artist, Freddy loved designing and decorating things, and she knew he'd have a ton of ideas about how they could make their sled truly stand out for the judges. Most of his ideas would probably be a bit *odd*, but odd could be good. They'd need to make sure their sled screamed PEACH, and if *anyone* could come up with ideas for how to do that, it was Freddy. She'd be happy to help him do the work of actually decorating it—and she knew Herb would love to help, too—but she really hoped

Freddy would have some big, bold ideas to design their family's dogsled.

"Now that you've got your sled picked out," Philip said with a wink, "do you want to learn how to drive it?"

6

DOGSLEDDING HERB

Herb had never put dogsledding on the wish list of things he would like to do sometime in his life, because he'd never imagined it would be something he'd ever have a *chance* to do. But now here he was, in *Sweden*, in a snowy yard filled with dogs. Dogs that he—Herb Peach—would get to lead on an adventure across a frozen wonderland. Just wait until the other kids in Mr. Andrus's third-grade class heard about *this* adventure!

"You'll both get a chance to drive a sled if you like, but I need you to listen carefully to my Sled Talk before I let you run a team," Philip said. "There are a lot of things you have to keep in mind when you're mushing, to keep yourself and the dogs safe."

For the next fifteen minutes, Philip talked through words they needed to know ("Whoa!" to get the dogs to stop; "All right!" to get them to go again; "Haw" to turn left; "Gee" to turn right) and showed them how to put the dogs in a harness and get them hooked up to the line. He explained where you stood when you were driving the sled and showed them how to get the sled to slow down on downhills to keep the dogs from running so fast they might hurt themselves. Then he showed them the special bar where they could stand, and the pad that dangled off the back of that bar that they would stand on to get the team and sled to stop and stay stopped. "The most important thing to remember is, *never* take your hands off the sled. If you lose control, you hold on—no matter what. If you let go of the sled and fall off, I can guarantee that the dogs aren't gonna stop and wait for you. They'll keep running and you'll be left alone."

Herb swallowed. He didn't like the sound of that.

"Just don't let go," Philip said again. After his Sled Talk, Philip began choosing a team to hook up to the line for Herb's first ride. One by one, he unhooked a dog from its chain and led it—barking and leaping—over to where Herb and Lucy were waiting with harnesses. They got to help Philip wrestle each dog into a harness and attached it to the line stretching out in front of the sled.

Philip was a patient and friendly teacher, and he let Herb and Lucy do lots of the work to get the dogs ready for their journey. The Santa look-alike would show them how each step in the process was done, then he'd let Herb and Lucy both try to do the same things all on their own. Once all the dogs were in position, Philip tucked a big, fluffy sleeping bag into the passenger/gear compartment in front of the sled handle and asked, "Which of you would like to help me drive the sled today?"

"I would!" Herb cried out immediately.

"Can I ride in there?" Lucy asked, pointing to the cozy warm area that stretched out in front of the sled's handle.

"Sounds good to me," Philip said with a nod. "Hop in and get comfortable."

Before they set out, Herb knew he needed to get to know the dogs he'd be working with. They would certainly need to trust one another if they were going to be a team. After spending the past six months or so training Great Aunt Lucinda's pups to listen to his instructions, Herb had learned that spending a little one-on-one time with each dog seemed to help a lot. So now, Herb greeted their team of sled dogs individually, giving each some ear rubs and a few encouraging words.

Herb was surprised to learn that the dogs didn't need to wear boots, the way he did out in the snow. "When it gets *really* cold and we're taking them out on long runs," Philip explained, "we do have some booties they can wear if the snow is getting balled up between their paw pads." But on regular cold days, Herb learned, the dogs' feet were either fine staying bare, or they got dipped in a special pot of waxy stuff that helped protect their paws from the frozen ground.

"Ready to set out?" Philip asked.

"Out where, exactly?" Lucy asked.

"Into the world," Philip said, pointing toward the gate that led out past the kennel.

Herb couldn't believe it. "We can ride the dogs and sleds outside the kennel yard?"

Philip laughed. "The dogs are going to be pretty disappointed if we got them all set up and don't let them truly run. It's not like a pony ride at a carnival; we don't ever just ride the sled around the yard."

Herb was excited but nervous. What if they tipped their sled? What if the dogs ran in the wrong direction? What if he fell off? Worse, what if he didn't fall off but the dogs wouldn't stop and they just *kept* running, until Herb and the dogsled team were all the way at the *real* North Pole? "Will you be with us?" he asked

Philip, suddenly a little less sure than he was a few minutes earlier.

"The whole time," Philip promised. "I'd trust you to drive it yourself, but I won't have you do that until you're ready. In any case, the dogs know what to do on the trails around here. You just need to learn to work with them and become familiar with the commands."

As soon as Lucy was settled into her compartment and Herb and Philip were positioned on the rails at the back of the sled, Philip unhooked the dogs from the rope that had been keeping them from running away while they got the sled ready. Then he joined Herb at the back of the sled, put one foot on the brake pad that dangled off the back of the sled and the other on the rail, and said, "All right!"

The moment they were released, the dogs on the line went silent and began to run. Philip helped guide the sled out of the yard and onto the snowy street. The dogs' tongues hung out of their mouths as they pulled the sled forward. Philip showed Herb how to put one foot on the pad that helped slow the team down, to keep them from going full speed right away.

They'd only gone a few slow blocks past the kennel yard before Herb spotted their dad standing outside a boring-looking single-story building on the outer edge of town. Dad was chatting with three other people who could have been men, women, or monsters (Herb found it was hard to tell who was under the puffy snowsuits everyone wore around town near the Icehotel). "Dad!" Herb yelled out.

Dad turned in their direction and waved. "Dad!" Herb called again. "Look at us! We're driving dogs!"

Philip signaled for the dogs to stop—"Whoa!"—and put his full body weight on the brake. As soon as the team was stopped, they all started barking and howling and yipping. Herb could tell his furry friends were disappointed to be stopped so soon after they'd set out from the kennel, but they were so well-trained that they all did as they were instructed. Herb thought about how naughty *his* pups would be if they were part of a sled dog pack, and vowed to double down on their training when their family returned home. How fun and adorable would it be if Dash, Donny, Vix, and Rudy could pull a miniature sleigh filled with stuffies through the backyard next winter?

"Look at you," Dad said, as Herb waved to him from his perch at the back of the sled on the street in front of the boring work building. "That sure looks fun."

"It is," Herb agreed. He got a better look at the group of people Dad was chatting with, and saw that one was a man, and two of them were women. They all looked friendly. "Do you want a ride with us, Dad?"

"Not just now," Dad said. "I'm actually just finishing up my meeting with the team here. This is Johan, Katia, and Eline—they're the three who will be traveling to the research station with me. We're working out final details for our trip up north this week. In fact, Herb, you'll find this fun—we actually get to ride with a team of sled dogs out to the research center when we go. One pair will take a snowmobile, but the other pair rides with a sled so we can get all our stuff out to the research station."

Herb tried not to look disappointed as Dad talked about his work trip. He knew his dad was excited to get a chance to visit this very special research center out by a giant glacier while they were on their vacation in Sweden. But if he was being totally honest, he didn't really want his dad to go. He worried about the danger of Dad walking around on a glacier (even though it sounded like it was pretty safe, and Herb had a feeling it was also pretty neat to walk on a giant slab of slow-moving ice). But more than anything, he kind of worried his dad would like the time he spent with these Swedish researchers *so* much that he would forget to spend any time with Herb and his siblings. This was supposed to be a family trip, and Herb didn't want to share Dad with anyone.

"We leave for the glacial research center tomorrow," Dad told Herb and Lucy. "I'm going to spend one night up there with the team of scientists, but will be back in plenty of time for the ice-carving contest and the final dogsledding race at the end of the Frozen Olympics."

"But what about the cooking competition and sledding?" Herb asked. "You're part of our team for those events, too."

"Yes," Dad agreed quickly. "I am. But I'm also part of a team who's going on this expedition at the glacial research station. Luckily, I'm able to fit in *both* things while we're here. And I'll get to be a part of the Frozen Olympics and other activities that take place today, before we leave in the morning."

"You *promise* you'll be home in time for the ice carving and dogsledding race?" Herb asked.

"I'll be home in plenty of time. I'm only going to be gone for one night, Herbie—two days. Promise. And Great Aunt Lucinda will take very good care of you while I'm gone."

"A promise is a promise," Herb reminded Dad. "Just one night."

Dad laughed. "One night. That's all. I wouldn't want to miss out on the rest of the fun." Dad's guarantee made Herb feel a lot better. Two days and one night. Dad would only miss a couple of events in the Frozen Olympics, and Great Aunt Lucinda could help fill in for him during the activities he'd miss while he was gone. Promises meant something, and Herb knew his Dad wouldn't dare to break one. A year ago, that might not have been true. But after the past six months of learning how to be a family without Mom, Herb knew his dad wouldn't ever let them down again.

"Let's let Dad finish up his meeting," Lucy urged. "I'm ready for our ride."

"Me too," Herb agreed. With a final wave to Dad and his three new scientist friends, Herb followed Philip's lead and eased up on the brake as he yelled "All right!" Then he grabbed tight to the sled rail and helped guide their team of dogs out into the freshly falling snow.

7

FROZEN GLOBE

Freddy had explored nearly every inch of the Icehotel grounds—both inside and out—and only had one final building to check out: the round theater building that sat majestically in the middle of a snowy tundra just outside the Icehotel's Ice Bar. Designed to look like Shakespeare's Globe Theatre in London, the small theater was built in the shape of a circle with an open-top roof. Earlier that day, Freddy had learned that it hosted nightly performances of shortened versions of Shakespeare's plays.

He'd been waiting all morning for the theater to open to guests, and finally—*finally*—Freddy spotted someone going inside. He raced after the person, catching the large door before it had closed all the way. "Hello?" he called out. The ice sculptures and walls inside the lobby caught his words and swallowed them up. *"Hej!"* he tried, testing out the Swedish version of "Hi," in order to appear friendlier.

"Who is it?" a voice called back in English. A woman with very dark hair and thick-lined eyes appeared from behind a snowy wall. "The show won't start for a few hours," she informed him.

"I know," Freddy said. "I just wanted a chance to look around. I don't really like theater, so I'm not going to come to a performance. But I wanted to see the building."

The woman raised her eyebrows and gave him a cold look. "You don't like theater?"

Freddy suddenly realized this was a bit rude. Maybe—probably—this woman was an actor in the show at the Frozen Globe, and it was possible he'd just offended her by declaring his dislike of theater. "It's not really my style," he confessed, since it was too late to swallow what he'd said. "I'm an artist, and probably my *art* isn't a lot of people's favorite thing, either. But that doesn't really bother me. Everyone's allowed an opinion, right? But the only opinion that *really* matters is the artist's own."

"You're an artist, eh?" she asked, gesturing for him to follow her. He did as he was told, letting the woman lead him into the large, open-air theater. In the center of the space was a stage, surrounded by a rounded audience seating area.

"Yep, I draw and I also like to build stuff," Freddy told her, skipping down the steps toward the stage. "Are you an actor?"

"Indeed," the woman said. "Can I ask you something?" And then, without waiting for Freddy's answer, she asked, "How do you know you don't like theater?"

"Watching a bunch of people stand around and talk on a stage is boring," Freddy said. "I've seen a few plays at school, and I guess I'd just rather spend my time doing other stuff. I'm Freddy, by the way."

The woman nodded, and said, "My name is Anna. It's nice to meet you, Freddy, even if you don't think you like theater." She ushered Freddy up onto the stage and turned him so he was facing out to the area where the audience would sit later that night. As soon as he was standing front and center, Anna asked Freddy, "How does it feel to be at the center of everything?"

It felt good, Freddy realized. He'd never stood on a stage before, and he felt pretty powerful up there. Unable to resist, he bellowed, "Helllllloooo!" at the top of his lungs. The sound bounced back to him from the edges of the theater. "That's fun."

Anna laughed. "Imagine how much *more* fun it is when the seats are all filled with audience members who are waiting for you to transport them to another world."

Freddy snorted. Anna had a fancy way of saying that actors told stories. Just like all other artists, they were storytellers. If only the stories actors told were *interesting*, he could get excited about plays. And don't even get him started on *musicals*! Those were even worse—a bunch of people just randomly starting to sing and dance about dinner or chores or whatever? No thank you.

"Freddy," Anna said. "I'd like to invite you to come by to watch a performance of our show tonight, and then stick around afterward to tell me what you thought of it. I think we might be able to change your mind about theater."

"I doubt that's gonna happen," Freddy told her honestly. "But sure, I guess I'll come."

"Here's another idea," Anna said with a laugh. "If you like it, I might be able to get you a chance to be a part of the show. We have quite a few battle scenes in the performance we're doing this month, and I could probably sneak you in and get you suited up in some armor to help with a battle or two on stage. You'd need to rehearse with us a bit, of course, but it could be a fun way to change your mind about live theater. Diving in is the best way to get a good taste for it."

Freddy's mouth dropped open. "Armor?" he asked. "Like, *real* armor?"

"Well, stage armor," Anna said, shrugging. "But it looks pretty real."

Freddy thrust his hand out. "Anna, my friend, you've got yourself a deal."

* * *

"An *actor*," Freddy blurted out to his family later, when they'd all gathered on the Icehotel's north lawn. It was almost time for the first event in the Frozen Olympics: the snowperson-building contest. The place where they'd met wasn't really a lawn so much as a giant field covered in snow. But Josef had told them to "gather on the north lawn" and this was where the FROZEN OLYMPICS banner was hanging, so it had to be the right spot. "I get to be an *actor* with the Icehotel's theater troupe!"

"That is so cool," Herb said, then he announced, "Guess what? I got to help drive a sled dog team today!"

"And I got everything set for my trip with the team up to the glacial research station," Dad boasted.

Great Aunt Lucinda smiled and tucked her curly, friendly grandmother wig further up under her fuzzy hat. "I had a lovely massage and sat in the sauna and had a warm cinnamon roll."

"Yay for all of you. But now . . ." Lucy said, all business. She glanced across the yard and stared down their competition.

Freddy followed her gaze and saw that Ellen and her super-duper-successful family were gathered in a clump, the big Banerjee family from Michigan was also nearby, as well as the dads and their twins. Freddy hadn't yet seen the mother-daughter team from Maine on the field, so maybe they'd decided not to participate. Fine by him; that would be one less group to beat!

"We need to make sure we build the most epic snowperson on earth," Lucy went on. "Because we have to have to take the lead in the Frozen Olympics so we can take Ellen *down*."

Freddy gawped at his sister. Lucy wasn't usually the

From the Sketchbook of Freddy Peach:

UPDATED
FREDDY'S HANDY-DANDY FROZEN
OLYMPICS COMPETITOR GUIDE

Two dad-dudes
Twin daughters

Weiss-Buckthorn Family:
Seaside B&B
Northern Washington

Old guy and lady
Dad-age guy
Boy – 6 or 7??

Banerjee Family:
Anderson's Resort
Upper Peninsula of Michigan

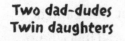

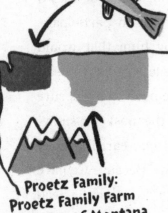

Proetz Family:
Proetz Family Farm
Mountains of Montana

Peach Family:
Peachtree B&B
Duluth, Minnesota

Parents
Ellen
Two brothers

Dad
Great Aunt Lucinda
Freddy
Lucy
Herb

Janice &
Janeen Murphy:
Cozy Cottages
Middle of Nowhere
Maine

Mother and daughter

cutthroat competitor in their family, so this announcement surprised him. "Um . . . okay?"

Lucy shrugged and explained, "She stole my snowsuit *and* took the best Ice Suite. I want revenge."

"I like it," Freddy told her. He was glad he wasn't
the only one who really wanted to win this Frozen
Olympics. It would definitely give them an edge if they
were all gunning for the big prize and worked together
for a victory. "It would be so cool if we actually come
out on top, and get an ice castle of our own built in the
backyard of the Peach Pit next winter."

Lucy clapped her hands. "Not *if* . . . when. *When* we
win the Frozen Olympics, Freddy."

Who was *this* Lucy, Freddy wondered, and what had
she done with his actual, real-world sister?

Josef called everyone forward and explained the
rules of how the Frozen Olympics would work throughout the week. "We'll assign three points to the winning
team for each challenge, two points to the runner-up,
and one point for third place. No points will be awarded
if you place fourth or fifth in a challenge." Freddy looked
around; still no mother-daughter team to be seen. Which
meant there would only be four teams total competing
in the snowperson-building competition. He definitely

did not want to be the only team to walk away with no points! That would be very embarrassing.

Josef continued, "The judging team will be made up of myself, Lo, and Anders." A young woman and the guy they'd met during their first night's meeting waved to everyone. "We'll award points based on creativity, level of difficulty, and your final result."

All of this made sense to Freddy. He was ready to get the show rolling! Icehotel staff had plowed mounds of snow into big piles for each team to use for their creation. With the amount of snow they had to use, Freddy realized they could probably build a snow ogre and still have plenty of snow to spare. As soon as the judges gave them the go-ahead, each of the teams raced to their family's work areas and got to building.

The snow was cold and fluffy, which made it hard to shape. Usually, the best snow for building stuff, Freddy had learned over years of playing in the backyard at home, was a little warmer—so it held more water. With snow this cold, they had to add some water to get it to be stickier, which made all the white stuff *also* stick to their mittens. After some discussion that morning at breakfast, the Peaches had decided together that they would try to play off the theme of that year's Icehotel and build a Snow King and Snow Queen. This had been

Great Aunt Lucinda's idea, and everyone else agreed that it was the perfect choice.

But after almost an hour had passed, the Peaches had nothing more than two big, snowy lumps to show for all their effort. After helping for a short while, Great Aunt Lucinda had now retired to a bench on the side of the yard, and was cheering them on with a cup of something warm in her hands.

Earlier that morning, Dad had insisted that they try to utilize the Scientific Method to get their creation built, which in practice went a little something like this:

1. Ask a question. (What are we trying to build? Snow Royalty.)

2. Do background research. (How can we build that? Um . . .)

3. Construct a hypothesis. (If we can just get the snow to stick to itself, we should be able to shape it exactly the way we want . . .)

4. Test with an experiment. (Here, kids, let me try this way! Or this way . . . or . . . like this?)

5. Is the procedure working? If no, repeat steps 1–4. If yes, carry on. (Short answer: Nothing worked as planned at any step of the process.)

6. Analyze data and draw conclusions. (Verdict: This is going so badly, it's almost as if we've never seen or touched snow before.)

7. Do the results align with the hypothesis? (No. This isn't as easy as it sounded.)

8. Analyze and communicate results. (Result: Not great.)

Lucy's analysis was clear—she was frustrated, Freddy knew—and she kept communicating their results by kicking the snow. Herb, meanwhile, was having a ton of fun throwing the fluttery snow into the air, then letting it sprinkle down on him. Freddy was stumped. "One hour to go!" Anders called out.

Freddy took this opportunity to look around the yard to see how some of the other teams were faring. The friendly Banerjee family from Michigan had created some sort of bridge out of ice. "Not a snowperson," Freddy muttered, thinking that not following the rules of the contest had to be a sure way to lose some points. But at least they had *something* built; that was more than the Peaches could say.

The dads and twins from Washington had created a single, sturdy, traditional snowperson—made of three varying sizes of snowballs—that was almost ten feet tall.

It had big oranges for eyes, black licorice for a mouth, a gnarled carrot for a nose, rocks for buttons, and was wearing a puffy Icehotel hat and a scarf. This snowperson didn't have much *style*, but again, at least it *existed*.

Ellen's family had somehow created a five-person *family* of snowpeople—each almost exactly the size of one member of the Proetz family. They'd divided and conquered, and now each member of the family was working to decorate one of the snowpeople on their own. "They made their *family* out of snow . . ." Freddy muttered, impressed.

"Come *on*," Lucy growled, kicking at the snow once again. "Why won't this snow just stick together and *do* something?"

The final hour passed far too quickly, and by the end, the Peaches had something roughly resembling two snow lumps (which Freddy decided to call monsters, to give them *some* flair). Each was wearing what was *supposed* to be a crown, but really, they just looked like lumps of snow on top of their heads.

The Peaches' experiment had failed—miserably. Freddy didn't even have to wait for the judging to know that they would be the ones walking away from the first Frozen Olympics event with no points at all.

FROZEN OLYMPICS
SCORE SHEET
· · · · · · · · · · · ·

Proetz Family Farm (Montana): 3

Seaside B&B (Washington): 2

Anderson's Resort (Michigan): 1

Cottages in the Middle of Nowhere (Maine):
   0 (no show)

Peachtree B&B (Minnesota): 0 (losers)

8

NIGHT ON ICE

After their disastrous loss in the first Frozen Olympics competition, Lucy was angry. Between Freddy's artistry, Herb's work ethic, her determination, and Dad's organization (and, of course, Great Aunt Lucinda's friendly encouragement from the audience), she really thought they would have done better. But they'd lost—badly.

"Do you not get much snow in Minnesota?" Ellen asked Lucy with a sly grin in the women's changing room later that night. They were putting on warm sleep outfits for their upcoming night-on-ice. After much discussion, the Peaches had chosen Herb's favorite—the animal room—to sleep in. They decided it was the Ice Suite that felt most like home, what with all the naughty ice animals sprinkled all over the place. And Lucy hoped that a carved-ice bed that looked like a fluffy dog bed would be slightly more comfortable . . . even though she knew it was unlikely.

"It snows a ton in Duluth," Lucy told Ellen grumpily.

"Oh," Ellen said, acting like this was a surprise. "It just seemed like your family didn't really know what to *do* with snow during the Frozen Olympics event today, so . . ."

Lucy glared back. She was trying to be kind, but it was very difficult to give Ellen the benefit of the doubt. Rather than saying something mean, Lucy quickly zipped up her snowsuit and skipped brushing her teeth—just so she could get away from mean Ellen Proetz.

For their night of sleeping inside the actual Icehotel, they'd been instructed to wear long undies, a hat, and mittens, but not to sleep in their snowsuits. Apparently, the sleeping bags in the Ice Suites were warm enough that Arctic explorers used the same kind! But until it was time to actually crawl inside her sleeping bag and go to sleep, Lucy was going to wear her snowsuit and keep as warm as possible.

After the snowperson-building contest that

afternoon, Lucy had thought she might never be warm again. But she'd taken a hot shower in their warm hotel room, and then the Peaches had all sat down together for a huge meal of stew (surprisingly yummy) and fresh bread. For dessert, they'd had a gooey, warm chocolate brownie-cake thing that was called *kladdkaka*, which means "sticky cake" in Swedish. It was the most delicious cake Lucy had ever eaten, and she'd made a note to ask the Icehotel kitchen if she could add it to their list of recipes back home. After dinner, Freddy and Dad had gone together to the Shakespeare performance at the Frozen Globe, while Herb and Lucy played cards with Great Aunt Lucinda inside the warm hotel.

Now, feeling warm and snuggly and surprisingly excited to sleep a whole night on a big slab of ice, she met up with her brothers and Dad inside their Ice Suite. Herb had already selected the bed that he and Lucy were going to share and had snuggled into his puffy sleeping bag. Lucy perched beside him and felt the bed. She was delighted to discover that—though the bed frame was made of solid, carved ice—there was a pair of reindeer skins resting on top of the ice that blocked some of the chill. Freddy informed her that the reindeer skins were like the insulation tucked into the walls of the Peach Pit, and would hopefully keep the chill of the ice from seeping through the mattress and up into Lucy's bones while she slept. There was also a regular feather pillow waiting for her on the bed, which would certainly make the night much more comfortable!

Dad and Freddy nestled into the other bed, side by side in their matching mummy bags. At Dad's request, Lucy snapped a quick picture of them, and also of Herb in the other bed, and then tucked Dad's phone deep into the pocket of her snowsuit for safekeeping in the night. Then she pulled off her snowsuit, piled it in a heap next to her bedside, and burrowed in next to her littlest brother.

"I'm beat," Dad said. "But this bed is surprisingly comfortable." Lucy sat up and glanced over at her dad and brother in their icy dog bed. Both had cinched their sleeping bags tightly around their faces, so only their mouths and noses were exposed to the cold air in their animal-themed Ice Suite. She giggled, thinking to herself that they looked like two giant, frozen burritos squeezed onto a chilly plate together, just waiting to be popped in the microwave.

"I'm tired, too," Freddy said, yawning loudly.

"Did you know it's only two in the afternoon back in Minnesota?"

"That's weird," Herb declared. "I'd be in reading time if I were at school." Then he rolled over to look at Lucy and said, "Will you read aloud?"

Lucy's hands were wrapped in big, chunky mittens and, while she was feeling surprisingly cozy inside her sleeping bag, she knew that pulling her hands out into the frozen air was not a great plan. "Maybe I can tell you a story instead?" Lucy suggested.

Dad rolled out of bed and hopped in his sleeping bag to the door, so he could turn off the main lights in their suite. Some warm, pale blue and pink night-lights glowed softly in each of the corners, which made the room feel warmer somehow.

Herb curled into a ball inside his sleeping bag and tucked his head under Lucy's chin.

"There once was a dog named Herb . . ." she began. Herb giggled and snuggled closer. "Who had always dreamed of racing with his pack to the very tip of the North Pole . . ."

While Lucy told her brother the story, she could hear Herb's breaths lengthening as he settled into sleep. In the neighboring bed, Dad was already snoring softly and Freddy's nightly rustling (just like a dog, he always had to wriggle and spin to find the perfect position before drifting off to sleep) had stopped. Slowly, Lucy's own voice began to waver. She tugged the hood of Herb's sleeping bag more tightly around his face, then did the same with her own. Soon, she'd drifted off into a deliciously sound sleep on her frozen bed of ice.

• • •

In the morning, Lucy was the first member of the family to wake up. She wasn't *certain* it was wake-up time yet, since the Ice Suite was just as dark as it had been the night before. But based on how awake she felt, she guessed it was probably daytime outside. She rolled over to face Herb, and was happy to see her little brother looked warm and comfortable atop his reindeer hide, and hadn't frozen into an icy Herb-cube at some point in the night.

She wiggled her toes, then stretched her legs out long. Her sleeping bag made swishy sounds in the cold, still air of their Ice Suite.

"Is that you, Lulu?" Dad whispered.

"Morning," Freddy muttered from the far side of the other bed. "I slept like a bear in hibernation." Then he added, "Did you know that when a bear hibernates for the winter, their heart rate drops to as low as eight beats per minute? And they go their *entire* winter sleep without peeing, even once?"

"I need to pee now," Herb blurted out. Obviously, he was also now awake.

Since they were all done sleeping, the four Peaches hustled out of their Ice Suite back to the heated changing rooms to use the bathroom and brush their teeth. Then, with their night on ice over, they headed over to the warm hotel restaurant to meet Great Aunt Lucinda for breakfast.

They had a couple hours to fill before the second competition in the Frozen Olympics—the cooking contest—began. Today would be another chance to win a point or three against Ellen's team in their family's quest to be named the Frozen Best, and Lucy was ready to redeem herself! Cooking was a Peach family specialty—they'd spent a whole summer baking and selling pies, after all—and their breakfast was always very popular with guests at the B&B. With Great Aunt Lucinda (who had developed the recipe for their family's famous peach pie) around to help, they were sure to win this one. They had to, or their chances of winning the final prize were almost nonexistent.

"So . . ." Lucy said, taking a sip of her hot cocoa. "What's everyone going to do today?"

"Well," Dad said, looking proud. "I head out soon for the research station up north. There are four of us going together. Since you can't get there by car or train or roads of any kind, two people will ride on a snowmobile, and two members of the team will drive a dogsledding team to help haul all our gear."

"Do *you* have to drive a snowmobile? Have you ever driven one before?" Freddy asked, cringing.

Dad shook his head and grinned. "No, but I'm sure it can't be any more difficult than driving a car or the Peach Pie Truck. If they need me to drive the snowmobile—or even the dogsled team, I suppose—I'm ready and willing!"

All three of the Peach kids looked at one another. Dad had not exactly been a natural at driving the Peach Pie Truck. Lucy hoped someone else in the group would be handling the snowmobile and dogsledding team, or they weren't going to get very far.

"I, for one, am excited for the Frozen Olympics cooking contest this morning," Great Aunt Lucinda said, obviously trying to get everyone to stop thinking about the danger of Dad behind the handles of a snowmobile.

"Me too," Lucy said. "I also want to make sure we start decorating our sled for the dogsledding race at the end of the week. We don't have a lot of time to make it perfect."

"Philip said I can maybe try driving a team of dogs on my own this afternoon," Herb announced. "If he thinks I'm ready."

"Wow," Dad mused. "Herb, that's wonderful." He turned to Great Aunt Lucinda and said, "Please be sure you get some pictures while I'm gone. I don't want to miss anything."

Sullenly, Herb said quietly, "Then maybe you just shouldn't go."

Lucy put her hand on Herb's and shook her head a tiny bit. She knew how excited their dad was about his trip to a glacial research station. She also knew Herb didn't like when Dad chose work over them. But she knew Dad had been trying so hard to find a balance between work and family the past few months, and he really wouldn't miss much during just one night away. "We'll have fun while he's on his adventure," Lucy whispered to Herb. "And just think—you might be driving a team of sled dogs all on your own by the time he gets back!"

"I'm going to start my ice-carving lessons after lunch," Freddy declared. "I want to practice tons before we have to do that contest in the Frozen Olympics." He took a big bite of soft-boiled egg and then blurted out, "Oh, and I almost forgot! I have my first rehearsal for the Shakespeare play after dinner. Anna said if everything goes well and I can figure out my cues and they can find me a costume that fits, I'll get to perform in a scene onstage with the theater troupe tomorrow night."

"What are cues?" Herb asked.

"It's a theater term," Freddy said loftily, even though Lucy was pretty sure he'd just learned what it meant himself. "A *cue* is an actor's sign that it's time for them to come onstage." He glanced at Dad and noted, "Make sure you get home before the show tomorrow night, okay, Dad? I don't want you to miss my big theatrical debut."

"That shouldn't be an issue," Dad assured him. "It sounds like we'll be home before dark, since it can be a bit dangerous to travel back from the research station at night." He glanced at his watch and said, "Well, kids, I ought to get going. I know they were eager to set off by eight this morning, and it's already seven thirty." He gave Lucy and her brothers each a quick half hug, then patted Great Aunt Lucinda on the shoulder. "I'll catch you all on the flip side!" he said, grinning.

"No, Dad," Freddy said, groaning at their dad's attempt to use a "cool" phrase. "Just no."

"In Swedish, you could say *vi ses*," Herb told them. "That means 'see you later.'"

"Well then, *vi ses*," Dad said, waving. "I'll see you tomorrow!"

Once Dad had left and they'd all finished eating their breakfast, Lucy, Herb, and Great Aunt Lucinda decided to spend the morning brainstorming ideas for what they might prepare during the Frozen Olympics cooking competition. They wanted to make something that showcased who they were as a family, but also something that they would be proud to serve to their guests at The Peachtree B&B. After talking about whether their best effort would be Cousin Millie's Apple Muffins, or Freddy's Welcome Cookies, or Dad's Dutch Baby Pancake, it soon became clear that the obvious choice was Great Aunt Lucinda's Famous Peach Pie. After all, it was the featured item in their food truck the past summer, and it included peaches— their family's namesake fruit! "It makes perfect sense," Lucy told the others. "How can we *not* win with our famous pie?"

"I agree," Freddy chimed in. Herb and Great Aunt Lucinda were also on board, but only after Herb convinced the others to let him cut the decorative shapes out of the top crust before they baked it.

But when they got to the kitchen for the start of the second event in the Icehotel's Frozen Olympics, they found out there was an important twist to the cooking competition: Each team was expected to incorporate some sort of *frozen* element into their finished dish, in honor of the Icehotel. And the food they presented to the judges would need to be served on a plate or dish made of ice. "Does it count if it's a food served *with* something frozen, like a ball of yummy ice cream on top of the main thing we make?" Freddy asked.

"If that's what you choose to do, that's fine," Josef answered. "But you will probably lose some creativity points."

"Ugh," Lucy grumbled. Their warm peach pie definitely wouldn't be as delicious if it were served cold on a frozen slab of ice, and the only way to incorporate something frozen into their dish would be to serve the pie with ice cream. "We could have gone with pie à la mode, but that's not really making the most of the frozen theme."

"And frozen *pie* is the pits," Herb said, frowning.

"So, now what?" Lucy moaned. "We can't afford to lose any creativity points."

"Now," Freddy said, sounding less optimistic than he usually did. "I guess we start from scratch and brainstorm some more and hope we can come up with a winning idea before we run out of time."

Kladdkaka Recipe

(Translation: Sticky Cake)

Preheat your oven to 180 degrees C
    About 350 degrees F!

In a medium-sized bowl, whisk together until
    smooth:
- 1 1/3 C sugar (you can add a little more or less,
    depending on how sweet you like stuff!)
- 2 eggs

Then gently blend in:
- 1/2 C flour
- 1/4 C cocoa powder
- Pinch of salt
- 1/2 C melted butter
- 1 T vanilla

Grease an 8-inch round cake pan (9-inch will work
    in a pinch) with butter. Sprinkle approx. 1 T
    cocoa powder over the butter to coat the pan.
    Pour in the cake batter and smooth it out (the

mixture will be very thick!). Bake for 20-30 minutes, or until the top of the cake is slightly hardened. The center of the cake should still be soft and gooey.
Let it cool for 10-15 minutes.

Sprinkle powdered sugar over the cake, slice it into pieces, and top with fresh whipped cream and/ or berries (optional).

YUM!

9

(FROZEN) PEACH PIE

Herb thought as hard as he could, trying to ignore the voices of all the other competitors who were squeezed into the kitchen alongside them. The Icehotel kitchen wasn't in the frozen part of the hotel (obviously), but rather in the basement of the warm hotel, nestled beside the dining area. It was a tight, cozy space filled with giant fridges and gleaming metal countertops and several large ovens and a huge, walk-in freezer filled with all kinds of wonderful foods and ingredients. All the sweepstakes winners—except Dad—had showed up to take part in this event (including the mother-daughter team from Maine, who had chosen to skip the snowperson event) which meant there were nineteen people total in the small kitchen, not including the judges. Herb was glad his family had had a summer stuffed in a food truck together to get used to cooking in tight quarters, since it was hard to even hear himself think in a space this full of people.

"We're going to need to get more creative," Great Aunt Lucinda said, clearly not at all frazzled by the frozen-food twist on the day's contest. "Since when do us Peaches let life's surprises knock us down?"

Freddy clapped twice and grinned, which perked Herb up again. If Freddy and Great Aunt Lucinda thought they could come up with a plan for this competition, he was on board, too. They'd dealt with much bigger surprises than this one and pushed through, that was for sure.

"So, what could we make that's frozen?" Lucy asked. "All I can think of is ice cream."

"Homemade ice cream is the obvious choice," Freddy agreed.

"And ice cream was Mom's favorite," Herb added. "Except for Great Aunt Lucinda's peach pie. That was Mom's *favorite* favorite."

"So, what if we combine them?" Great Aunt Lucinda said, her eyes bright and sparkling under her friendly grandmother wig (she'd told Herb she chose this one today because it made her look like Julia Child, a famous chef!). "We could create peach pie ice cream."

"Ooh," Herb said, grinning. "That's a good idea!"

"We can take all the components of our peach pie and fold them into a homemade vanilla-and-cinnamon ice cream," Freddy said excitedly. "We could even bury little chunks of crust in there, and peach filling, and—"

Herb cut him off to say, "And the crust won't have to be as perfectly formed if it's going to be chopped up anyway, so maybe I can help make it this time!" During their summer road trip in the Peach Pie Truck, Herb had discovered he wasn't very good at making piecrusts. There was an art to it, and Dad was really the only one who was any good at rolling them to the correct thickness and making sure they were large enough—but not *too* large—to fill the whole pie pan. During their food truck adventure, Herb had gotten frustrated, not being able to help bake with the family, so he'd invented Herb's Cinnaballs. These were just little chunks of piecrust dough that were rolled in butter and sugar and baked until they were flaky and crusty and yummy. "Little tiny versions of Herb's Cinnaballs would be the perfect thing to blend into our ice cream!"

"You're right, Herb," Lucy agreed. "You can make Herb's Cinnaballs to blend into our ice cream. Great Aunt Lucinda, maybe you can make the peach filling, since it's your pie recipe, after all? And Freddy and I can try to figure out how to work the ice cream machine."

Herb was excited he had been given his very own job, and got right to work blending the butter, flour, and sugar to make a perfect crust dough. The other teams were working on their own recipes nearby, but Herb tried to tune everything else out and focus only on what his family was doing. Lucy was hard at work beside him, blending up a homemade ice cream mixture, and Freddy was carefully studying the ice cream machine to figure out how to get it to churn out frozen delicious-ness. Great Aunt Lucinda hummed softly as she mixed frozen peaches, sugar, lemon juice, and spices to create the messy slurry that usually filled the inside of their family's signature pie.

The time passed quickly, and soon they were stir-ring together Lucy's runny ice cream mixture, Great Aunt Lucinda's peach filling, and even more cinnamon to make a perfect peach pie–flavored ice cream soup. Herb popped his Cinnaballs in the oven——they'd decided to mix the chopped-up crust chunks in at the very end, so they wouldn't get soggy (no one liked soggy crust!).

As soon as his main job was finished, Herb suddenly had a *brilliant* idea. He nudged Great Aunt Lucinda in the side and said, "What if we formed our ice cream into a pie shape? You know . . . like an ice cream *cake*, but a peach ice cream *pie?*"

Great Aunt Lucinda beamed at him. "Herbie Peach, you are a genius. That would be a very cute way to present our dish."

The ice cream machine took some time to get rolling, but when it did, the contraption worked like magic, transforming the messy, sloppy mixture into a beautiful sunset-colored frozen delight. Each member of the family tasted a little spoonful, and Great Aunt Lucinda declared it "almost perfect." Then she sprinkled in a little more nutmeg, a dash of cardamom, and finally tossed in Herb's cooled chunks of crust bits. Finally, they mixed the whole mess together until it was just melty enough that they could form it into a pie pan.

Once they had it all pressed into the pan, they popped their creation into the deep freeze to make sure the whole thing would freeze solid, and relaxed. Herb took this chance to look around and see what everyone else was cooking. The mother-daughter pair had also created something out of ice cream, but they seemed to be crafting a *seven*-layer cake, complete with four different flavors of ice cream, and three other layers that looked to be different types of crumbled-up cookies and/or cream. They'd built the cake itself, and now they were crafting a pair of moose antlers out of hardened chocolate. "Whoa," Herb whispered. Seeing the Maine ladies' more elaborate ice cream creation made Herb nervous about the Peaches' chances at winning.

"That's really something," Great Aunt Lucinda noted. "You know what we could do?" she said mischievously, grinning at Herb and his siblings. "Maybe we could make some little dog prints in the top of our ice cream pie, in honor of my little treasures at the Peach Pit."

Freddy whooped and got to work carving a stamp of a dog paw out of a chunk of solid white chocolate.

The dad-and-twins team from Washington State had prepared a dish that looked like oysters on a bed of ice. The oysters themselves weren't very creative, Herb thought, but the girls had added some sort of homemade Popsicle-looking thing on the side. Herb didn't know much about oysters, but he was pretty sure they were a salty food and judging by how it looked, he guessed the Popsicle was sweet. It seemed like kind of an icky combination, if Herb was being honest.

It looked like the Banerjee family, from Michigan, had tried to build a big, hollow ball made of clear ice to hold their food inside. It was a super-clever idea, but the thin ice ball was *too* thin and had split in half, so now it was just two domes of ice that looked ready to collapse at any second. Under each dome was a pile of what looked like slices of steak. Herb wasn't sure what was going on with their dish, but was relieved he wasn't one of the judges who had to taste that cold, slimy-looking beef creation.

Ellen's family was bickering over a bowl of what looked to be some sort of cold blueberry soup. What a clever idea, Herb thought! But then he overheard Ellen say it "tasted like vomit mixed with cough syrup," and this made him giggle and feel like maybe they had a chance at winning a point or two or maybe even three!

Just before the judges announced that time was up, Lucy carefully pulled their ice cream pie out of the deep freeze. She cut three thick slices, carefully slid each onto a carved-ice plate, and then Freddy used his dog print stamp to press little dog prints on the top of each slice. Herb then used his brother's carved stamp to track dog prints out of melted frozen peach juice across each of the icy plates. It actually looked like a little dog had run across the dishes! Finally, Great Aunt Lucinda put a dollop of cinnamon whipped cream on top of each slice and declared their masterpiece "Perfect!"

Herb was so nervous during the judging that he couldn't even focus on all the things the judges were saying about the foods that had been created. When it came time for Josef, Anders, and Lo to check out his family's frozen peach pie, Herb held his breath and waited to see what they would say. "Amazing," Lo declared, smiling widely after her first bite. "It actually tastes like peach pie, but it's frozen! I love the little chunks of crust you've hidden in the ice cream."

Herb beamed happily. That part was his addition!

"And the little paw prints," Anders said, laughing. "How cute."

"We have four dogs who live with us at The Peachtree B and B," Herb explained. "We wanted to be sure they were also included in our signature dish." Herb watched a lot of British cooking shows with his friends at the Birch Pond retirement community, and he'd heard the contestants on those shows use words like "signature dish" a lot. He also knew that cooking competition judges usually liked to know the reasons behind a chef's choices, which is why he'd explained the dog prints on their plates and pie. He hoped it would help when it came time to award creativity points.

"Wonderful," Josef said with a belly laugh. "That's an excellent addition."

When the judges were ready to announce the winners, Herb squirmed into the comfortable spot between

Great Aunt Lucinda and Lucy. "In third place, getting one point," Lo began, "is the Weiss-Buckthorn family!" Looking around, Herb realized this was the fathers-and-daughters family from Washington who had created the oyster-and-ice-pop dish.

"And in second place, receiving two points today," Josef said, winking at Herb, "is the Peach family, with their Frozen Peach Pie!"

"Two points are better than no points," Freddy said quickly.

Herb noticed his sister glancing over at Ellen's family. Ellen glared back, a disgusted look on her face. *Yeesh,* Herb thought, *maybe she had too many bites of her family's vomit soup.*

"And the winner of today's Frozen Olympics competition," Anders said, pounding a wooden spoon on one of the shiny metal countertops, "are Janeen and Janice Murphy, whose chocolate antlers and seven-layer frozen dessert proved to be absolutely unbeatable."

The mother-daughter team hugged each other tightly and jumped up and down excitedly. Herb had to admit that their layered ice cream dish really did look most impressive of all the entries. And if that cake *tasted* half as good as it looked, they deserved to win. It reminded him of a winning dish from one of his cooking

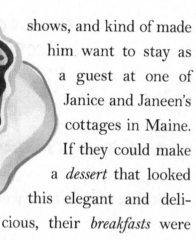

shows, and kind of made him want to stay as a guest at one of Janice and Janeen's cottages in Maine. If they could make a *dessert* that looked this elegant and delicious, their *breakfasts* were probably amazing.

"Two points isn't three . . . *but* we now have two more points than we had yesterday at this time," Freddy said, grinning as they began to clean up their station. "Peaches, with us and the mother-daughter team now on the scoreboard, the Frozen Olympics are officially anyone's game."

FROZEN OLYMPICS
SCORE SHEET
. . . .

Proetz Family Farm (Montana): 3

Seaside B&B (Washington): ~~2~~ 3

Anderson's Resort (Michigan): 1

Cottages in the Middle of Nowhere (Maine): ~~0~~ 3

Peachtree B&B (Minnesota): ~~0~~ 2

10

STAGE COMBAT

After the cooking competition was over, everyone dispersed to do their different chosen activities. Great Aunt Lucinda headed off to have tea with the mother-daughter team from Maine, while Freddy followed Lucy and Herb to the kennels. He wanted to check out the sled their family would be riding in during the final event of the Frozen Olympics, so he could start to think about ideas for how to decorate it with a truly Peach flair. After checking out their chosen sled and letting Herb introduce him—by name—to several dozen dogs, Freddy headed back out alone into the snow and ice. He had big stuff on his agenda for the rest of the day: first, an ice-carving lesson; *then*, he was meeting Anna and some of the other Frozen Globe cast members to practice for his big stage debut as a real Shakespearean actor!

As promised during their ride in from the airport, Josef was one of the people in charge of the ice-carving lessons. Freddy was excited to spend some one-on-one time with Josef, since he seemed to be full of fun facts about the Icehotel and Freddy wanted to ask him a million questions. But when he showed up at the ice-carving studio, he was dismayed to find Ellen and her two brothers were already there. So much for alone time.

"Oh," Ellen said, rolling her eyes. "*You're* here."

"Yep," Freddy said cheerfully. "Good observation. I see you're here, too. Remind me of your names again? I'm Freddy."

"Ellen Proetz," Ellen said, gesturing royally to herself. Then she pointed at her younger brother and said, "That's Finn." She flicked her chin in the direction of the older brother. "And that's Levi."

"Nice to meet you," Levi said, seeming slightly less chilly than his sister.

"Are you hoping to get a little practice in before the ice-carving competition?" Ellen asked. "Since you seem to be the only one from your family showing up for the lesson, it's going to be three Proetzes against one Peach, which will probably make it hard for you to win this one."

"That's okay," Freddy said. "I'm not taking a lesson just because I want to win an event. I also think it will be super-cool to learn, for fun. I love building stuff—I have a whole art shed where I build sculptures and projects and stuff back at home—but I've never tried to make something out of *water* before."

Ellen gave him a weird look. "It's not water. It's ice."

"Ice is water," Freddy pointed out. "Same tool, just in a different form."

"Whatever," Ellen said. Neither Finn nor Levi said anything at all.

Josef came bustling into the chilly studio and greeted them all. *"Valkommen!* Welcome!"

He got the four of them settled at their stations, giving them each a big slab of ice that looked like a massive ice cube. Then he handed out some tools and supplies: sharp chisels, a giant pair of tongs, a compass (the kind they sometimes used in Freddy's dreaded math class), a massive (and heavy!) apron, safety goggles, giant gloves, and a little brush. Freddy rubbed his hands together, waiting for the chainsaw and other power tools. But Josef brought nothing like that around, and Freddy soon realized the tools they'd be using were just regular old tools—much like the stuff they'd used when they were renovating the Peach Pit that past fall.

Josef explained a few basic things about ice carving and showed them some tricks for how to find the art that he promised was hidden within each of their blocks. The way he talked about it made Freddy think of this one time, before Mom died, when he'd gotten a Geologist Kit for Christmas. He got to pound away at a block of hard, solid sand with chisels and a little hammer, and as he chipped away at the solid block of sand, he'd found a bunch of hidden jewels and pretty rocks inside. Since he could see *through* the ice he was going to be carving,

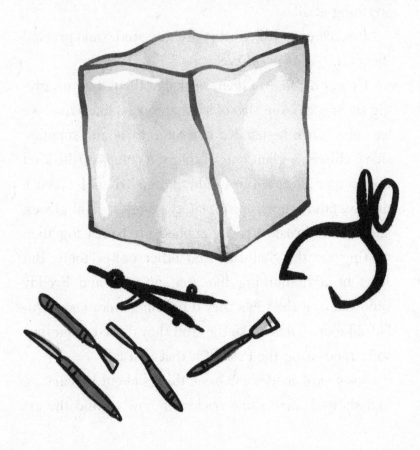

he knew there probably wasn't actually anything hidden inside the ice—but Freddy liked imagining that there were jewels and other treasures just waiting to be uncovered.

This gave him an idea for what he'd like to try carving out of his first block of ice: a crown. How hard could it be? Maybe he'd make *two* crowns! How excited would his little brother be if Freddy came out of his ice-carving class with a special, Freddy-made ice crown for Herb to wear around inside the Icehotel that night? They could sit in the thrones in the Great Hall and pretend to be in charge! Maybe a special crown would help Herb be less sad about Dad being gone at the glacial research station for the night. He couldn't wait to show his brother what he'd made, just for him.

Josef gave Freddy and the other three students some pointers on how to get started and explained that they needed to chip away at the ice slowly, so as not to remove too much right away. "I'm here to help guide you if you need it," Josef said. "But you need to learn to work with the ice, so I don't want to get too involved. Practice makes perfect, and it's your project." Freddy could tell it would be slow and tedious work—just like the Peach Pit mansion renovations had been—but he was certain he was up to the challenge. He would turn this boring, blank ice into something beautiful!

"A crown, eh?" Josef said, laughing, when he stopped by Freddy's station and Freddy told their teacher his plan. "That's . . . a lot. Are you sure you don't want to start with something a bit *simpler*? Say, a giant *jewel* from a crown?"

"Nope," Freddy said, shaking his head. "Go big or go home, I always say. I want to make the whole crown, or nothing at all. But I think I can figure out how to do it. And if I can't, well . . . practice makes perfect. It's just ice, right? There's always more to be found outside if I need to start over and try again."

"Okey dokey." Josef nodded. *"Lycka till, min van."*

"Licka whatta?" Freddy said, studying his chisels and other tools to try to figure out which one he wanted to use first.

"It means, 'good luck, my friend' in Swedish," Josef told him, laughing.

As it turned out, Freddy needed much more than luck to make his ice crown work. What he really needed was a lot more skill than he currently had. The *luck* (and safety tools) Josef had offered him only went so far as to prevent him from chopping off his own finger. By midafternoon, when Freddy had to leave the ice-carving studio for his meeting with the theater actors, he basically had nothing more than a big, deconstructed, colorless slushie resting on the cold work slab in front of him.

Unlike other art forms he'd tried (paint, clay, found-object building projects) the cleanup from ice carving was fairly simple—he just swept all his shaved ice mess into a big bucket and laid his tools on a special table to dry. Then, with a promise to return the very next day to try again, Freddy skipped out into the bitter cold to make his way to the theater.

When he arrived at the Frozen Globe, Anna was waiting for him onstage. "Are you ready?"

"Absolutely," Freddy said, hopping up and down to try to warm his icy toes. Even though the ice-carving studio was heated to a warm and comfy thirty degrees Fahrenheit (just two degrees below the temperature where water freezes, Freddy noted), the air down at floor level was cold enough that his toes had frozen inside his giant moon boots. He'd been standing still for so long that his feet had sort of lost all feeling. Now that he was moving again, his toes had begun to tingle and then prickle as they began to thaw. "So, where do we start?" he asked Anna.

"I'm going to teach you some basic stage

choreography," Anna said. "I think it's important that you understand how we are able to create the illusion of fights and battles onstage without anyone getting hurt."

Freddy nodded agreeably. Though he'd had plenty of practice doing pretend battles with his best friends during Cardboard Camp each summer, Freddy had noticed that they used *real* weapons onstage when he'd watched the performance the night before. Hitting someone with a metal sword was a whole different thing than bopping Ethan or Henry over the head with a cardboard weapon.

First, Freddy got to choose a weapon of his choice that he would use in battle. He was offered a sword and shield, a big battle-ax, a mace, a dagger, a spear, and a rapier, as well as a few other weapons he would need to look up later. After studying them all carefully, Freddy decided that the battle-ax looked like it would be the most fun to swing round and round. It was a weapon fit for an ogre! But a moment after he'd lifted it up and off the table of weaponry, he decided he wanted to go with something a little more classic, sophisticated, and flashy—so he chose the sword and shield instead.

"A great choice," Anna told him. "You strike me as a sword guy."

"I do?" Freddy said excitedly. This was possibly the nicest thing anyone had ever said to him.

"It suits you," she confirmed. "You also look like the kind of person who could handle a longbow, but it's much more fun to learn stage combat with a sword."

Once that decision was made, for the next hour or so, Freddy, Anna, and a couple other cast members worked together to learn some of the basic fight moves Freddy needed to perfect before he'd be allowed to go onstage with the actors to perform. He was given a battle partner he'd be paired with during the show itself—a twenty-something Norwegian guy named Oystein, who looked like he'd been dropped onto the stage directly out of one of Freddy's illustrated Norse Mythology books.

While other actors worked on their movement training nearby, Freddy and Oystein practiced their own special set of choreography—*choreography* was the fancy word for all those preplanned body, feet, arm, and weapon movements they'd follow during their scenes—onstage together. After just a few minutes, Freddy had to strip off his snowsuit, since he was sweating heavily. For the first time since they'd arrived in northern Sweden, Freddy was actually *hot*. Stage fighting was hard work! Anna watched, cutting in every few seconds to adjust their feet and arms and bodies this way and that, until Freddy's head was so stuffed full of instructions that he thought he might burst.

"Let's stop there for today," Anna finally said, much to Freddy's relief. He wasn't sure how many more steps he could remember, and his thighs felt like they were on fire from all the lunging he'd been doing.

"Nice work," Oystein said, clinking his sword against Freddy's like a high five. The force of his sword tap nearly knocked Freddy over, which made him glad he and Oystein wouldn't be fighting for *real* onstage.

"You too," Freddy said, clinking back.

"We'll see you tomorrow, yes?" Anna asked. "You will have another rehearsal—next time, in your costume and armor—and if all goes well, we can bring you up onstage to perform these scenes with us tomorrow night."

"Cool," he said, slipping his snowsuit back on. "Thanks so much. I'll see you guys soon." Then he tested out the new Swedish he'd learned from his brother that morning. *"Vi ses!"*

As he made his way through the sharp, blowing snow outside the Frozen Globe, he muttered to himself, *"Freddy Peach, Shakespearean Actor."* Obviously, their good luck hadn't dried up yet. He couldn't *wait* for his family—especially Dad!—to see him performing his very own scenes with professional actors in an important, famous play on a huge and fancy stage made of ice. They were going to be so proud!

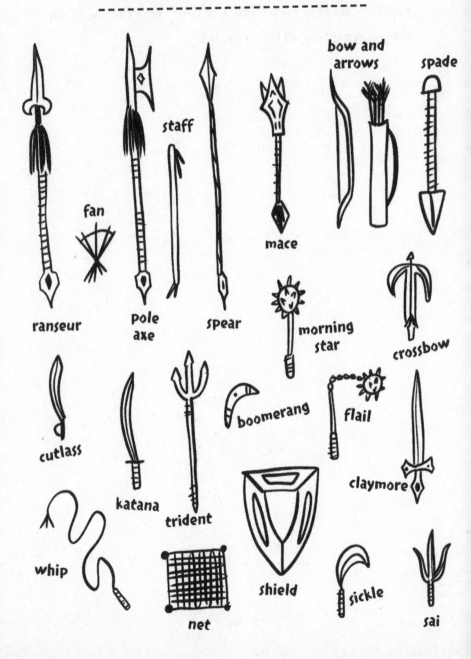

From the Sketchbook of Freddy Peach:
WEAPONS TO CHOOSE FROM

11

MAGIC SKY

Lucy had spent the better part of the afternoon helping Herb and Philip feed and harness dogs for various dogsledding trips Icehotel guests had signed up to go on. Herb was obviously very much in his element at the kennel, and the dogs all seemed to love him. But try as she might, Lucy couldn't seem to get the hang of the harnesses—they always ended up tangled when she touched them, and both Lucy and the dog she was dressing would wind up frustrated—so Lucy was leaving.

While Lucy had studied their sled for the competition, trying and failing to come up with a clever way to decorate it, she had gotten to witness Herb helping Philip put tiny harnesses on the litter of sled dog puppies. They didn't get to pull anything just yet, but Philip had explained that they had to get used to the idea of wearing their harnesses early in life, so that it would feel more comfortable and natural to them when they got older and got to practice joining the team. Herb had convinced Philip to let *him* try a harness on, too, and then Herb spent much of the rest of the day wearing his own sled dog harness around while he did his kennel chores. He looked adorable, if a bit uncomfortable.

Lucy waved goodbye to her brother, asked Philip to ensure that Herb got back to the warm hotel safely, then zipped up her puffy snowsuit and headed out into a brisk wind. There were plenty of frigid days in Duluth during the winter (and sometimes in the summer, too!), but somehow the cold air at the Icehotel felt different. With only her nose and eyes poking out of her warm layers, Lucy wandered around the little town-like area that surrounded the Icehotel.

As she walked around the charming little winter village, she couldn't help but think about how much her mom would have loved this place. Mom had been a *huge* fan of Christmas romance movies that always started showing on TV each year just after Halloween, and before she died, she had even started to let Lucy watch some of them with her. Lucy remembered that, at the time, she didn't like any of the mushy stuff in those movies—luckily, there wasn't *that* much kissing in them—but she loved that special time with her mom. Mom would make a cup of tea for herself, and a cocoa for Lucy, and then they would curl up under a blanket on the couch together and groan as they watched silly and improbable love stories set in very fake-looking towns.

There were lots of big things Lucy missed about her mom, but it was the little things that were hardest to live without. Watching movies and cooking shows together, going for walks and talking about Lucy's day, coming up with silly crafts to do on a boring Sunday. Her mom had liked to work on those adult coloring books, but she'd always get bored after filling in the first corner and would leave the rest for her family to fill in. She never even cared if Herb—who was still so little when she died—took a colored pencil or crayon or Sharpie and just scribbled all over the whole page, ignoring the lines altogether. Those memories of her mom were some of the things she missed the most.

Lucy headed toward the giant Icehotel, trying to decide which of the offered activities would have been most interesting to her mom. She would do whatever *that* was this afternoon, she decided. It was just a matter of figuring out what Mom would have most wanted to do during a trip like this.

She wove through the Icehotel's lobby, passing by

groups of tourists who had come to check out the frozen palace during the day. Lucy overheard someone say, "You'd have to be crazy to sleep inside this thing." She smiled to herself, thinking about how proud she was that her family—her slightly *crazy* family—had slept there the previous night and none of them (not even Dad!) had freaked out. It had been cold, and slightly uncomfortable, but that night on ice would be one Lucy would remember forever. These were the kinds of new family memories she was trying to sprinkle into the empty and colorless holes that were left behind when Mom died.

Freddy was still planning to spend the rest of his nights sleeping inside different rooms of the Icehotel, and he had already chosen The Outer Space Suite to sleep in tonight. Lucy, Herb, and Great Aunt Lucinda were all planning to sleep in real beds inside the warm hotel, and Lucy couldn't help but worry a little bit about her middle brother spending the night inside a room at the Icehotel alone. But before he left for his work trip, Dad had said it was okay with him, and Lucy knew she had to trust him and his decisions. Their dad hadn't been reliable or really even very present for a couple years after Mom died, but now that he had started to figure some stuff out, Lucy knew she could trust him to be the parent again.

Lucy wandered into The Outer Space Suite and found Ellen and her brothers were already in there. "Oh," Lucy said. She held up a hand in a wave. "Hey, how's it going?"

The Proetz kids all muttered something that was possibly a greeting, possibly a growl. "*We're* sleeping on ice again tonight," Ellen announced regally, out of the blue. "Our parents are letting us stay in a different Ice Suite than the one we slept in last night—*alone*."

"That's cool," Lucy said. "Freddy's doing the same thing. He's actually sleeping in this Ice Suite tonight." Then, for lack of anything else to say, she ran her hand across the reindeer hide on the bed in The Outer Space Suite and added, "These ice beds aren't as bad as I was expecting them to be. But it's kind of weird to sleep in a hotel made of ice, right? Like, sort of claustrophobic?"

"Not really," Ellen said. She narrowed her eyes and said, "*You're* not staying in the Icehotel again? Your brother's the only one who can handle it?"

"No, I'm n—" Lucy began to say no, that she was planning to sleep in the warm hotel with her littlest brother and their great aunt. But suddenly, she didn't like the idea of Ellen thinking she was some sort of wimp. "No, I'm definitely not going back to the warm hotel tonight. Why would I? I mean, we are here to experience the *Icehotel*, right? Why not make the most of it?"

A voice inside Lucy's head told her to stop talking. What was she *saying*? She'd had her one special night of sleeping on ice, and now she was very much looking forward to a warm pillow, and a bed she could read in before falling asleep, and relaxing under her fluffy pile of blankets in the morning while she woke up in total coziness. But knowing Ellen and her brothers were sleeping in one of the Ice Suites every night . . . well, how could Lucy *not*? That alone was like a little victory for the Proetz family. Lucy could not let them beat her in a game of toughness! "So, I guess I'll probably see you in the changing room later tonight," Lucy added weakly.

The three Proetz kids left, and Lucy slumped down on the bed. The chill of the ice platform seeped through her snowsuit and long undies, and she suddenly felt cold and miserable. She wasn't sure what it was about Ellen Proetz that bothered her. But she *did* bother her, and Lucy didn't like that she'd allowed this random girl to irritate her, like a sliver of wood that was stuck deep inside the skin of a finger.

Was it because Ellen had been so unfriendly to Lucy on that first day (as a B&B owner, she should know—better than *anyone*—how to be kind to strangers, right?!)? Or was it because she was her family's competition in the Frozen Olympics? Lucy couldn't help but wonder if maybe it was both of those things, but also maybe it was because Ellen's family was built a lot like her own family had been . . . back when their mom was still alive. Maybe Lucy felt a need to prove to everyone that a family *without* a mom could win, just as easily as one *with* a mom might?

As Lucy threaded her way through the icy hallways, looking for answers in the frozen art and trying to figure out what activity she might try that her mom would have loved, she bumped into Great Aunt Lucinda. "Lucy!" Great Aunt Lucinda said, seeming just as surprised to find her great niece roaming the halls of the Icehotel as Lucy was to see her spa-loving aunt away from the warm hotel. "I'm just having another little look-see around these beautiful art suites, and then I've signed up for a nighttime snowshoeing tour out in the woods. Would you care to join me? They promised me it's an easy walk, and said we might see the Northern Lights."

"That sounds great," Lucy told her. Great Aunt

Lucinda had been such a blessing to their family over the past few years. She'd helped to fill some of the emptiness, some of the biggest, deepest holes their mom's absence had created in the center of the family. Great Aunt Lucinda wasn't a perfect—or even close—substitute, but as Lucy and her brothers started spending more and more time with her after Mom's passing, Lucy had begun to realize that her warm hugs and outgoing personality helped fill a little of the space that was left so glaringly empty and lonely without Mom in their lives.

Lucy and her great aunt headed back to the warm hotel together to get an extra layer of clothes, and Great Aunt Lucinda brought Lucy into the restaurant for a quick bowl of warm soup and a slice of rye bread to hold them until a late dinner. They swung past the kennels to let Freddy and Herb know where they were heading (Lucy was thrilled to see that Freddy had started to sketch up and play around with ideas for their family's dogsled design!), and made plans to meet them for dinner in the hotel restaurant at eight.

Once they were bundled up, she and Great Aunt Lucinda headed to the equipment room to get snowshoes and set out into the night. Janice and her daughter Janeen, from Maine, were coming along with them, as

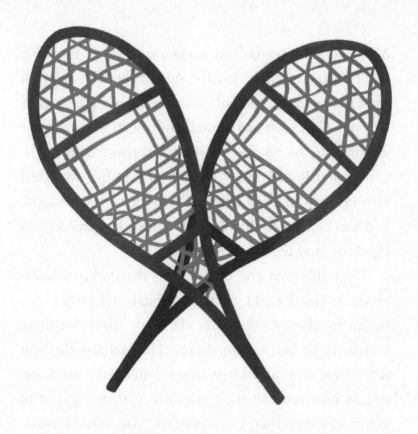

well as a few other hotel guests who Lucy hadn't met. Josef would be their guide, and he showed them all how to get suited up in snowshoes and gave anyone who wanted them a pair of poles for extra stability on the walk (Lucy passed, but Great Aunt Lucinda blurted out an eager yes).

Outside, the sun had long since set and the flickering twinkle lights in the trees were once again as magical as a painting—or "Main Street," from any one of

Mom's small-town holiday romance movies. The group trailed after Josef around the side of the Icehotel, past the Frozen Globe, and out into the untouched landscape beyond. They each had a small lantern attached to their waistbands, so no one would get separated from the group, and Josef had a headlamp to lead the way. He'd also brought along a Bluetooth speaker of some kind, and was playing traditional Sami music to remind them of whose land they were crossing.

Lucy followed the others into the dark, unfamiliar, snow-filled world. As they walked, and Lucy's eyes began to adjust to the dark, she could make out more and more of her surroundings. They passed through a forested area, and Lucy stopped suddenly when she caught movement in the trees nearby. Reaching out to get Josef's attention, Lucy pointed. "Ah, yes," he whispered. "Reindeer."

"*Real* reindeer?" Lucy asked. "Like, *wild* reindeer?" She knew her brothers would laugh at her if she admitted this aloud, but until she saw them when they arrived at the Icehotel, she'd always kind of thought reindeer were a made-up creature. Like unicorns. Or mermaids. She'd only recently discovered (thanks to one of Freddy's fun facts) that *narwhals* are a real thing (she'd always assumed those were made-up creatures, too!).

"Very real," Josef said. "I'm sure there are many of them. They travel in herds, so when you see one or two, you often know there could be ten, or even as many as a hundred."

"Whoa," Lucy said. She was also a herd creature, she'd discovered. Much as she loved sitting and reading alone in her reading fort or up in the Peach Pit's secret attic space, she was happiest when she was with her family. Lucy had learned that they all brought out the best in one another when they worked as a team. She wrapped her arm through Great Aunt Lucinda's, and together they watched as first one reindeer, then several more wove through the trees and disappeared into the inky blackness.

When the snowshoeing group got to a large clearing, Josef stopped them and told everyone to stand in a circle together, facing outward, and turn off their lanterns. At first, Lucy was nervous. What if they couldn't see anything, and Josef left, and they were stranded out here with no idea of where to go to get back to safety and warmth? But she trusted him, even after knowing him for just a few days, so she did as she was told. The others also flipped off their lanterns, and Josef flicked off his headlamp and music, leaving them all in hazy blackness and quiet stillness.

But after a moment, Lucy's eyes adjusted to the dark and she began to see stars. Millions and millions and millions of stars, all winking and twinkling and glowing from above. There were no buildings or trees around them, so looking up, it felt to Lucy like she was standing under a dome or inside a planetarium, with the sky stretched out like a blanket fort overhead.

Lucy wished, more than anything, that her mom could have seen this. She would have loved the interplay of nature and science and art, and how all those things came together to create a sky so beautiful you might almost think it was fake. Sometimes, at times like this, Lucy wondered if her mom was sort of keeping an eye on them and delivering these beautiful little surprises as her way of saying *hello,* and maybe even *I love you, and want you to remember I will always be with you in your heart.*

The longer they stood there, surrounded by stars and swirling snow and the sounds of silence, the more the cold began to soak through their layers of clothing and dig into Lucy's core. But it was worth it.

Far too soon Josef told them it was time to start moving toward home again. "Before you turn into frozen Peaches," he joked to Lucy and Great Aunt Lucinda.

But just as Lucy and the others went to turn on their lanterns, the edges of the sky lit up with a blaze of green that looked like someone had taken a paintbrush and swiped it across the bottom half of the sky. A moment later, there was another stroke of green and soon, the whole horizon was dancing with colors—dozens of shades of green, blue, and purple. It was the Northern Lights! Lucy had never seen them before, except in photographs at the art gallery in Canal Park back home.

"Did you know," Lucy said, parroting a fact she'd learned from her brother for the other people in their group, "the Northern Lights happen when electrically charged particles from the sun get carried into Earth's atmosphere? They collide with gases and then the gas particles and electricity create this special energy that shows itself as colors in the sky."

"You've done your homework," Josef said, making Lucy flush with pride. He added, "We get to see the Northern Lights more often in polar regions, because Earth's magnetic field pulls the particles to the poles."

"Mom would have loved this," Lucy whispered to Great Aunt Lucinda. "It's the perfect collision of art and science."

"A person might almost wonder if," Great Aunt Lucinda whispered back, "perhaps your mom is partially responsible for this. This is the kind of magic and beauty I like to believe Madeline had the power to create, and it's times like this that I wonder if maybe she's with us in spirit more often than we know."

Lucy smiled, watching as the crisp Arctic sky performed its dance of many colors. She liked to think and hope and believe that maybe, probably, Great Aunt Lucinda was absolutely right.

12

SLIP-SLIDING AWAY

After sleeping the previous night in their chilly Ice Suite, Herb had really enjoyed returning to the comfort of his warm hotel bed. It was very hard to get up on their third morning at the Icehotel since Herb just wanted to burrow a little deeper and stay snug and warm inside his double layer of blankets. But as soon as he remembered that today was the day of the Frozen Olympics downhill sledding race, Herb popped up and out of bed like a kernel of popcorn.

He and Great Aunt Lucinda had been the only two who'd slept in their warm hotel room the night before, since both Freddy and Lucy had decided to spend another night sleeping in an Ice Suite. Herb and Great Aunt Lucinda had had a wonderful night together, just the two of them. Herb had gotten a big double bed all to himself, and Lucy let him curl up with both pig and duck for the night.

After a late dinner the previous evening, Freddy and Lucy had headed off to the changing rooms together. Herb didn't think Lucy looked very excited about spending another night in a sleeping bag, but she insisted she would be joining Freddy in his quest to spend *all* of their nights in Sweden in the real Icehotel.

Meanwhile, he and Great Aunt Lucinda went up to their cozy room where his great aunt made Herb take a hot shower, but then as a prize, she let him pick the channel they watched on TV. The show was in Swedish, but it was a cooking show and Herb quickly realized cooking was easy to understand in any language. He'd fallen asleep while watching a competition about cakes.

"Who ended up winning the episode?" Herb asked Great Aunt Lucinda as he got dressed the next morning. His great aunt was sitting in front of the mirror adjusting her wig and applying her face.

"That chatty lady with the short hair," Great Aunt Lucinda said, glancing at Herb in the mirror. "From what I could tell, the quiet, tattooed man didn't finish decorating his cake on time, but if he had, I'm pretty sure he would have won."

"Today is the downhill sledding race," Herb said excitedly. "And I get to go on a long dogsled ride with Philip today. We're going to see a pretty church that's far away, and you can only get to it if you walk or take sleds or snowmobiles. There aren't any roads, just like the research station where Dad slept last night."

"That sounds fun," Great Aunt Lucinda said. "But I'm going to be honest, Herbie: I'll need to sit out the downhill sledding race. My hip is a little sore after snowshoeing last night, and I suspect I'll be a bit of a liability if I'm riding in a sled with you."

"You won't be a liability," Herb promised her, remembering that the word *liability* meant someone who was a burden, or problem, or might cause them to be at a disadvantage in the race. The sledding race was set up so that each group could compete as individuals in single sleds, or as a family in one big sled. Herb wanted his family to race as a team, but he seemed to be the only one who didn't want to compete alone. "It won't be as fun without you."

"I'll cheer loudly from the sidelines," Great Aunt Lucinda said. "I promise."

Herb didn't like to see anyone left out of anything, but he also didn't want to see Great Aunt Lucinda get hurt. She *was* kind of old, and if she fell out of a sled, well . . . Herb didn't like to think about that possibility. He was already worried enough about his dad up at the research center in the middle of nowhere; he didn't need to worry about Great Aunt Lucinda being in danger, too. "Dad comes back today!" Herb said excitedly, changing the subject.

Just then, Lucy and Freddy came barging into their warm room. Freddy immediately buried himself under a pile of blankets on Herb's bed, and Lucy mumbled something about defrosting her body in a hot shower. Herb pulled the blankets away from his brother's face and asked, "How was your second night sleeping on ice?"

Freddy groaned. "I think there's a reason they suggest people only spend *one* night sleeping inside the frozen rooms at the Icehotel." He tugged the blankets back over his face and in a muffled voice said, "I'm exhausted."

"Are you going to move back into the warm hotel tonight?" Great Aunt Lucinda asked. "Your dad is due home later today, so you can share his room again."

"Not a chance," Freddy muttered. "I made a vow to make the most of the Icehotel, and I don't break promises. Especially promises I make to myself. Tonight it's my turn to sleep in The Queen's Suite, either alone or with Herb or Dad or Lucy. Even if I leave here a *frozen* Peach, I refuse to wimp out!"

Herb and Great Aunt Lucinda shared a smile in the mirror. Freddy was nothing if not determined, and once he'd set his mind to sleeping in a frozen hotel room every single night of their special sweepstakes-winning trip, it would take some sort of catastrophe (like the Icehotel *melting*) to make him go back on his vow to himself.

As soon as Lucy was out of the shower and she'd dried her hair into a massive, fluffy pouf with the hotel's hair dryer, the four Peaches made their way to breakfast. While they ate fresh rolls with salted butter and homemade raspberry jam, they talked about their plan for decorating their sled for the final dogsledding race at the end of their week.

"Here's what I've been thinking," Freddy said. "We make a bunch of giant peaches—out of what, I don't know, but it will need to be something light—and turn the sled into something that looks like a giant pie pan. So, when we're riding in it, we look like we're baked into the pie. We'll be a giant Peach pie, gliding through the snow!"

Herb gaped at his brother. How did Freddy come up with this stuff? "I love that," he declared.

"Super on-brand," Lucy agreed. "It fits the theme of our family and The Peachtree B and B . . . I love it, Freddy."

"But the big question is, how do we build the peaches, and what do we use to make the pie pan that doesn't weigh much and also doesn't stick out the sides and catch the wind while we're riding?" Freddy plopped this challenge onto the table, making it clear that he was the *idea* guy, but had no intention of figuring out how to actually make his idea work.

"Could you ask some of your theater people if they have stuff we could use from their prop room?" Great Aunt Lucinda suggested.

Freddy pointed at her. "You are a genius," he garbled, his mouth stuffed with bread. "This is one of those times it pays to make new friends. I bet Anna and Oystein and the others will totally be willing to help. And, hey, here's another fun idea! What if we all carried swords and armor in the sled with us during the race?"

Lucy furrowed her brow. "Um, why weapons and armor?"

"We'd look fierce," Freddy said simply. "We could basically drape ourselves in furs from the theater's costume closet, and hold up stage weapons, and as the dogs charge through the snow, we could holler and yell and wave our weapons around to scare off all our competition."

"Let's focus on the *pie* theme first, okay?" Lucy suggested. "We can talk about furs and weapons later?"

Herb giggled. The image of their family, all dressed in furs and battle gear and holding weapons, while sitting inside a giant pie pan—it would be funny. He could just picture Dad in a big fur vest, swinging a giant Viking hammer or something. Suddenly, he couldn't wait for his dad to come home from his work trip later that day. He missed him. Herb and his siblings hadn't spent a night away from Dad in a really long time, and Herb didn't like his family to be separated. He wondered if Dad was missing him, and guessed that he probably was.

After breakfast, the four Peaches headed out to the small hill that would be the site of that morning's Frozen Olympics race. Josef, Lo, and Anders were already there, and had a big collection of wooden toboggans, plastic sleds, flying snow saucers, and even a couple of plastic trays from the restaurant's buffet line. "Pick your vehicles, Peaches!" Josef said, gesturing to the collection of snow vessels. "Then grab a helmet and feel free to test out each of the sleds before the race begins. You can give each one a trial run, and decide if you think you'll be faster as individuals or in a group sled. Even if you race as individuals, we'll only count the fastest sled from each family when it's time to award points."

Herb looked to the hill and noticed that the big, friendly Banerjee family from Michigan was already there. Several members of the family—the grandma, the dad, and the boy who was a little younger than Herb— were all riding down the hill separately on their own sleds. The grandpa gestured to Great Aunt Lucinda, and offered her a spot on a hay bale he was using as a seat to watch the action unfold.

While the Peaches scanned their sled options, the Proetz family arrived and began their own hunt for the perfect winning sleds. Ellen quickly nabbed an old-fashioned toboggan and began to drag it up the hill alone. Her brothers chose a flying saucer and a tray and followed her. The Proetz parents chose a regular plastic sled and laughed as they set off to ride down the hill together. Things like this always made Herb feel sad. He could imagine how much fun it would be to have his mom here for a race like this; he was sure she would have wanted to share a sled with him, and whether they won or lost, Herb knew there would have been lots of laughter during their adventure. But without Mom *or* Dad there, Herb was forced to grab a flying saucer that fit only *one* butt, and chased after his siblings (Lucy dragging a plastic sled; Freddy hauling a toboggan) as they made their way up the hill.

The hill they would be racing on for the Frozen Olympics was wide and treeless, so there wasn't much risk of running into other people or objects during the race. This was good. Once, when his school went sledding during gym class in first grade, Herb had crashed into one of his classmates while he was riding *down* and she was walking back *up* the hill. The quiet and friendly girl, whose name was Ruby, had gone flying up into the air and landed on the back of her head on the hard-packed snow. A teacher had to take her to the emergency room, and it turned out she'd gotten a concussion. Herb had felt so guilty about his fault in that accident that he hadn't gone sledding since. He was relieved they were wearing helmets today; he hoped that meant no one would leave the race with a concussion.

At the top of the hill, Herb shimmied into the center of his flying saucer, tucked his legs crisscross-apple-sauce, and rocked his body to scoot his sled right up to the very edge, where the hill started to slope downward. After taking a deep, icy breath for courage, he used his arms to give himself a little push from behind. Slowly, he began to glide down the slippery racecourse. He wrapped his mittened hands around the handles on each edge of the saucer and leaned back just enough that he wouldn't summersault forward and land on his face. As always, he got a tummy-drop feeling as his speed increased, and his eyes prickled as the wind slapped at his face as he soared through the bitingly cold air. His saucer was fast—almost too fast for Herb's comfort— and he was at the bottom of the hill in what felt like three seconds.

He looked up and saw that Lucy's sled had tipped halfway down the hill and she was sprawled like a star-fish in the center of a snow patch. Herb stared at her, his heart pounding, willing her to please get up and be okay. When she gave him a thumbs-up, Herb felt so relieved. Meanwhile, on the other side of the hill, Freddy was still trying to figure out how to maneuver his fancy toboggan, so he also hadn't gotten very far down the hill yet either. Herb felt proud, realizing he'd chosen the swiftest style of vehicle for himself. He wasn't used to winning very often when they had competitions within their family, and this small victory went a long way. Herb trudged back up the hill and took another ride down, all before either of his siblings had managed to reach the bottom for the first time.

After taking a bunch of test runs on each of the different vehicle options, the three Peach kids all found the sled that best suited them: Herb stuck with his saucer; Freddy went with a long, blue plastic sled; and Lucy chose a toboggan (she liked that it was steady, if a bit slower to start than some of the other options).

Like the Peaches, the Proetz family had decided to race in three different vehicles. Ellen had chosen a saucer, like Herb, the brothers were riding together in a toboggan, and the parents had stuck with their large plastic sled. The dads and twins from Washington had split up, with one father-daughter pair riding together in each saucer. The Banerjee family from Michigan had decided to pile *everyone* in their group into one giant, bright red plastic sled. "All this weight will shoot us down the hill extra-quick," the grandma said, taking up the rear of their sled. Then her adult son climbed into the front, and the boy plopped into the cozy-looking space between his dad and grandma. After their cooking competition win, the mother-daughter pair from Maine had chosen to sit this contest out.

Anders joined the competitors at the top of the hill. "Remember, only the fastest sled from each family will be considered when it's time to figure out our winners. So even if, say, all of the individual Proetz family sleds finish first, second, and third"—Herb saw Ellen shoot Lucy a smug look when Anders said this—"only the *first* of their family's sleds to finish is eligible to win points for their family. Make sense?"

Everyone lined up at the top of the hill, giving themselves plenty of room to spread out, hoping to avoid any mid-race collisions. "The first sled to cross the finish line"—Anders pointed to the bottom of the hill, where Josef and Lo had spray-painted a long, hot-pink finish line in the snow—"gets three points in today's competition. The second sled, from a different family, will get two points. Third, one point." He clapped his big leather mittens together, making a loud slapping sound. "Are you ready?"

"*Ja!*" Herb yelled in Swedish, as everyone else yelled, "Yes!"

"Take your marks, get set"—Anders raised his hand in the air, then dropped it down to his side—"and go!"

Herb pushed himself off the edge of the hill as hard as he could. He rocked forward, trying to build some momentum to get himself onto the hill and down to the finish before anyone else. Out of the corner of his eye, he could see that Ellen had started her descent and was even with Herb, but her brothers had already slid farther down the hill. Lucy was moving slowly, but steadily, way at the back of the group—Herb heard her call out from behind him, "Go, Herb! Win it for the Peaches!" Herb glanced over his shoulder and saw that Freddy was stuck at the top of the hill; Herb had a feeling he'd trapped the sled's rope underneath his plastic sled, and now his vehicle wouldn't glide through the snow at all.

Just as Herb started to pick up some speed and began truly sailing down the hill toward what he *hoped* would be a Peach family victory, he saw the big family from Michigan whoosh past him. All three generations were cheering and hollering, and their sled was picking up more and more speed by the second. The finish line wasn't far, so Herb leaned forward, knowing he couldn't let them beat him now. At this point, unless some sort of miracle struck, he was the Peaches' only hope for points!

Herb rocked his upper body forward in his saucer, hoping that a little bit of a lean would give him the added speed he needed. But almost as soon as he'd tilted forward, Herb realized he'd leaned too far. Before he could shift *back* in his saucer to fix his balance, Herb felt himself flying forward—up and off the front of his saucer. His face splatted onto the ground first, and Herb felt the sharp, needle-like snow bite into the little patch of exposed skin on his face. After his glorious face-plant, Herb rolled and clattered down the hill—his big, puffy snowsuit and helmet absorbing most of the impact—and finally came to a clumsy stop just a few inches shy of the bright-pink finish line.

Herb groaned, touching his mitten to his face to wipe away the snow that had stuck to his skin during the fall. The snow came away pink with blood from what Herb *hoped* was just a bloody nose or a little scrape. He hoped he hadn't lost a *tooth* or something (unless it was a baby tooth, and then he wouldn't really care since maybe the Tooth Fairy brought kids different stuff in Sweden!). But it didn't feel like any teeth were missing, and when he licked them, his lips didn't seem to be bleeding. Herb looked to the other side of the finish line and saw that the friendly sled team—made up of Grandma, Dad, and boy—from Michigan had already crossed the finish line, and so had the big toboggan with Ellen's brothers. Groaning, Herb rolled onto his saucer on his belly and used his feet to push himself over the finish line. "Third?" he croaked, wiping away a little more pink snow. "Did I come in third?"

Great Aunt Lucinda and Josef both raced toward him with a towel (Josef) and a warm hug (Great Aunt Lucinda). "You got third, Herbie," Great Aunt Lucinda said, checking him over to be sure there weren't any major injuries. The blood flowing from his nose had already slowed, but Herb definitely wasn't feeling like a million bucks. He felt like someone who had been hit square in the face with a bunch of sharp, freezing, hard-packed snow daggers. Great Aunt Lucinda chuckled and pulled him in closer. "That, my dear, is what I'd call a hard-earned point."

Just as the two father-daughter saucers came gliding slowly past the finish line, Freddy and Lucy ran the rest of the way down the hill to meet Herb at the bottom. Herb collapsed into his family's arms, smiling despite his still-bloody nose and stinging face.

One point was a whole lot better than none.

FROZEN OLYMPICS SCORE SHEET

• • • • • • • • • • • • • • • • • • •

Proetz Family Farm (Montana): 3 3 5

Seaside B&B (Washington): 2 3 3

Anderson's Resort (Michigan): 1 1 4

Cottages in the Middle of Nowhere (Maine): 0 3 3

Peachtree B&B (Minnesota): 0 2 3

13

BATTLE PLANS

After the downhill sled race, Freddy grabbed a quick snack in the hotel dining room with his siblings and then set off to meet his castmates onstage. Meanwhile, Lucy brought Herb to the dogsledding kennel to get some much-needed love and care from his dog friends. As soon as he got to the theater, Freddy got suited up in a costume the crew had chosen for him, and then he and Oystein worked on their choreography and fight scenes together for nearly two hours—until Anna declared Freddy "stage ready."

"Yes!" Freddy whooped. "So, I can perform tonight?"

Anna laughed. "You may."

"I can't wait for my dad to see the show again," Freddy told them, carefully putting his weapons and costume away. "But this time, with *me* in it. He's going to be totally impressed."

"Be here promptly at six, if you intend to go on tonight," Anna told him. "We do a quick vocal warm-up as a cast, and then get into costume just before curtain."

Curtain, Freddy had learned, was when the show officially started. There wasn't *actually* a curtain around the Frozen Globe stage, but he'd been asking some of his castmates to help him learn theater words. If he was going to become an actor, he'd need to be able to play the part like a pro!

Before he left the theater building to head over for his next lesson at the ice-carving studio, Freddy and the show's prop master—a *different* guy named Anders—went to the theater's prop shed to see if there were any fun things the Peaches could use to decorate their sled for the Frozen Olympics dogsledding race. The prop closet was like a giant, walk-in treasure chest; it was filled with old set pieces and various strange items that had been used onstage during previous shows at the theater, and a whole lot of dusty costumes and armor and broken weapons.

Freddy pulled a bunch of different things off the storage shelves, then hauled everything outside into a big sled so he could pull it over to the kennel later.

There obviously wasn't a huge pie pan, or a peck of giant peaches, but there were a few things Freddy thought they could maybe use to help build something that would work perfectly for this purpose. He grabbed a couple of long strips of thin, flexible metal they could attach to the sides of the sled to create a rounded edge that would make their vehicle look like a pie pan. He also found a massive basket-like thing that Anders told him had been used as a giant fairy bed in a production of *A Midsummer Night's Dream* once; Anders said he could use it however he wanted, because it was so old that it didn't need to be returned. It was a weird collection of stuff he'd grabbed, but in his builder's mind, Freddy could see how they could possibly pull these miscellaneous items together to create their pie sled without sacrificing any speed.

Just as he was leaving, Freddy spotted some huge paper-mache bird eggs resting on a shelf way up high. "Can I have these?" he asked Anders, already envisioning how a lot of peach-colored paint and little glued-on stems and maybe some leaves would turn these lightweight, pastel eggs into perfect peaches to nestle inside his pie pan.

"I don't see why not," Anders said with a shrug. "I didn't even know these were back here."

Freddy loaded his arms full of the giant eggs, feeling proud of his haul. He had always been pretty good at digging junk out of hidden places and turning it into something useful. After covering his sled-load of decorating supplies with a large tarp to keep it from getting coated with snow before he could pick everything up and pull it over to the kennel later, Freddy made his way to the ice-carving studio. Lucy was waiting for him at the door. "I didn't want to go in there without you," she said. "Ellen's inside."

Freddy rolled his eyes dramatically enough that he knew Lucy saw it. "Why do you let her get to you so much?" he asked.

"Why *doesn't* she bother you?" Lucy snapped back. "She's obviously out to get us."

"Okay," Freddy said calmly. "So, who cares? We can't control her or do anything about the way she acts toward us, and letting her drive you crazy isn't going to make it any easier for us to win, right? If you let her bug you, you're just giving her more power." Freddy had heard his art teacher, Mrs. Fig, say something to this effect once during class. He'd liked the way it had made him feel, and he liked the idea that he truly only had the power to control *himself* and the way he reacted to situations. Through his art, and his actions, and the way he responded to the world, he of course *hoped* he sometimes made an impact on how other people thought and acted, but ultimately, the only person he could *truly* control was Freddy.

"Fine," Lucy huffed. Together, they headed into the studio for another practice session before the ice-carving competition. Freddy led Lucy toward the carving station he'd worked at the day before and helped her get tools and gear ready in the station next to him, one that was already all set up with a big, fresh block of ice waiting to be carved. He could feel Ellen watching them from her post across the room, but Freddy just whistled and worked, kept his eyes on his own business, and tried to keep his sister distracted.

"It's good to have you joining us today, Lucy," Josef said. "And welcome back to the rest of you. I'm glad all of our sweepstakes winners have had a chance to come by to learn a few things about ice carving before this event in our Frozen Olympics!" After another quick lesson and a short demonstration—wherein Josef quickly and easily chipped at his block, transforming it into a puffy, frozen bird in about five minutes—Josef told them all that they could start to play with their tools and see what kinds of masterpieces their big, square blocks of ice might be hiding. He came over to Lucy's station and walked her through

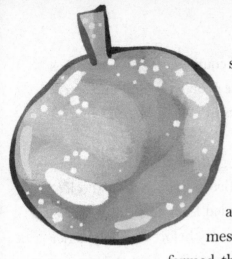

some of the basic techniques he'd shared with Freddy and the Proetz kids the day prior.

While Josef spoke, Lucy began to gently chip away at her ice. Freddy watched, mesmerized, as his sister transformed the chunky, square top of her block of ice into a perfectly rounded surface. "How did you *do* that?" Freddy asked quietly, as soon as Josef had wandered off to check on the others. "And so fast?"

Lucy turned and studied Freddy's block, which already looked like something a beaver had been chewing. The whole top half was shaved into frozen bits, and there was absolutely no shape to the remaining block of ice at all. "What did you do to yours?" she asked him, laughing softly.

"I chipped. And chiseled. And chopped," Freddy said, holding his hands over the remains of his ice.

Lucy snorted and gently tapped at her own ice. Freddy studied her block more closely, and realized she'd left a little chunk of ice sticking out of the top of her now-rounded block. "What's that?" he asked, pointing.

"A stem," Lucy said. "I tried to leave a leaf on it, too, but I got a little carried away with my chipping," she said, giving Freddy's pile of shaved ice another meaningful look. Then she added, "It's going to be a peach. I'm practicing for tomorrow's contest."

Freddy grinned. "That's perfect," he whispered, moving his body to hide Lucy's creation from their competitors, who were working on their own ice carvings across the room. "If you can make something like this during the ice-carving competition, I think we'd have a real shot at winning the next contest in the Frozen Olympics."

"I bet I probably can," Lucy said. Freddy knew his sister was both determined and talented; if she thought there was a chance they could win the next event in the Frozen Olympics if only she could figure out how to master ice carving, well . . . she'd stay here and practice all night if she had to.

"Oh!" Freddy said. "I just got the *best* idea. Maybe you could carve a *few* frozen peaches that we could add to our sled decorations? I got some stuff to build a bunch of super-colorful peaches out of old prop eggs that I found in the theater, but if we combined those with a bunch of icy, frozen peaches in our sled-pie pan, that would be so cool-looking. A combo of warm and cold, color and ice!" Freddy was even more excited now. "I'll help carve some of them, if I can figure out how to work my tools anytime soon. . . ."

Freddy trailed off as Lucy suddenly took a giant metal mallet and smashed it down on the beginnings of her frozen peach, turning the rest of her block into a crumbling pile of frozen shards. "Oh no!" she cried out.

"What are you doing?" Freddy shrieked, spinning around to see that Ellen, her brothers, and Josef were all gawping at Lucy and the shattered remains of her sculpture. "Why did you destroy it?" he asked in a hushed voice. "It was so good!"

"Protecting our battle plan . . . and destroying theirs," Lucy explained with a sneaky smile. Then she waved Josef over, pulling him away from helping Ellen, and said desperately, "Sorry, Josef, but I think I'm going to need some more lesson time with you."

Freddy sunk down on his stool and sullenly poked a chisel at his own block of ice. He wanted the Peaches to win the Frozen Olympics more than anything; Lucy, however, suddenly seemed to care more about making sure Ellen's family *lost*. These were two very different goals, and he had a feeling his sister had forgotten which one they should be focusing on.

He caught Lucy glaring at Ellen and her brothers across the room as she swept the remains of her icy peach into a bucket. She leaned in toward Freddy and whispered, "Never let the enemy know your strengths, Fred, and never tell them which way you're going to attack. This isn't just some fun, Frozen Olympics to me anymore; this is *war*."

From the Sketchbook of Freddy Peach:

ICE-CARVING DESIGN IDEAS

"SOPHISTICATION"
by Licherd Baklava

"SLUG"
by Bobby Samuria

"TURTLE"
by Micherd Baklava

"ROCK"
by Lil Tim

"TREE"
by Richard Baklava

"MELTED"
by Sichard Baklava

14

DOGSLEDDING THROUGH THE SNOW

Despite a scabbed-over nose, bruised cheek, and ice burns from his sledding incident earlier that morning, Herb was having one of the best days of his life. After nabbing a hard-won point for his family in that morning's downhill race, Herb had spent the rest of the day helping Philip in the sled dog kennel. Philip trusted Herb the way no one else in his life ever had (except maybe Bernie at the Birch Pond retirement center, who treated Herb like a real coworker); he let Herb tackle tasks that seemed like they would be reserved for an adult, and if Herb was having any trouble figuring the job out, Philip didn't just take over—he explained to Herb what he was doing wrong and then let him try again. Which meant Herb was actually learning stuff about how to care for sled dogs, and he *loved* it.

Herb had always assumed he would become a scientist, like both his parents, when he grew up. He was good at math, and he loved the science units in third grade (after spring break they would be studying snails that had been shipped to Minnesota from somewhere far away!). But after training Great Aunt Lucinda's pack of pups at home, working with the sled dog pack in Sweden, and excelling at his job taking care of the fish and turtles at Birch Pond, Herb was starting to think maybe he should consider some sort of career with animals. He knew he was *not* cut out for the kind of job where you *test* weird products on animals; rather, he wanted the kind of job where he could help animals have a happy and fun life. Maybe he would become a vet!

After feeding, cleaning hay, and helping to harness dogs that had been selected to go out with several groups of sled dog adventurers—as well as playing with the four-month-old pack of puppies much of the day—Philip told Herb to help him get a special team of dogs ready for a run out in the woods. "It's time for you to try driving the team on your own," Philip told Herb. "I saved some of my favorite dogs for us to take out on an adventure."

"Really?" Herb asked, incredulous.

"I'll ride along, of course," Philip assured him. "Just

in case something strange were to happen. But I trust you to handle the team all on your own. You've been out with me enough now that I think you know the commands and how to handle the pack."

Somehow, Herb wasn't even nervous. He'd been on several short rides with Philip, and now he'd spent so much time with the dogs and all their gear and equipment in the kennels that he felt like he really *did* know what he was doing. After getting the dogs ready, he and Philip suited up in extra layers and chose one of the sleds that wasn't being decorated by any of the Frozen Olympics competitors. Soon, they were zipping down the town's main street and then heading out onto the wild trails beyond. The dogs ran quickly, leaping and racing through the snow.

After they'd gone a few miles out from the Icehotel, Philip turned in the sled and told Herb to settle the pack and bring them to a stop. "Whoa!" Herb yelled out confidently, putting all his weight on the brake. The dogs did as they were told.

Up ahead, Herb could see a little red building jutting out of the bright white snow. A small, green, wooden cross made it obvious that this was the church Philip had promised to show him. The colors of the little building were a stark contrast to the blinding white snow and

the brilliant blue
of the sky,
and Herb was
sure he'd never
seen anything so wonderful
in all his life.

They carried on, and after riding a bit farther, Philip hollered out, "You might want to know that this is part of the course you'll follow during the dogsledding race on the final day of the Frozen Olympics." He winked. "I hope you've been paying attention during our ride."

Luckily, Herb *had* been paying attention. He'd been paying very close attention during their journey, because deep down, he had been a little bit nervous something might happen to Philip during their adventure, in which case he'd need to find his way back to the Icehotel all on his own. Even though he knew it was very unlikely anything would happen to Philip, Herb couldn't stop himself from thinking about the *what-ifs* in most situations.

Sometimes, these *what-ifs* were wonderings that he had about good things—like, *what if* his family had suddenly gotten *another* million dollars by winning the scratch-off lottery ticket they'd bought at a gas station during their summer food truck road trip. Or *what if* his dad let him keep the family of mice he found while he was cleaning the Peach Pie Truck.

But most of the time, Herb's *what-ifs* were worries. Herb had become a worrier when Mom died. Worrying wasn't ever fun, but for Herb, there was one good thing that came of it: His worries tended to make him extra observant. He noticed and paid attention to things, including a lot of stuff other people might not see. Herb had found that the more he focused on little details and held on to important information and treasures in his heart, and mind, and in his boxes of collections, the less time he had to fret about stuff. And somehow, paying attention and noticing the small things around him gave him more control over his big worries.

Herb's worrying had started when Mom died, because he'd been oh-so-nervous about losing his memories of her. And then he had begun to worry about something happening to Dad, and that had spiraled into worrying about Lucy and Freddy and his friends and lots of little things, too. He didn't *want* to worry about things, but sometimes he couldn't help himself. Today, his worry had caused him to pay attention to their route, and it turned out this was a good thing. Sometimes worry *what-ifs* had a good side.

"This is the *exact* route of the final Frozen Olympics competition?" Herb asked, now worrying that his family might be disqualified if anyone found out he'd gotten a sneak peek at the racecourse.

"Not *exactly* the same route," Philip said with another wink. "I wouldn't want to be accused of helping you cheat, even if you are my favorite family here. But having spent some time riding out here, Herb, you'll definitely feel a bit more comfortable when we set the course and send you out with your team of dogs and a map."

"Have you given any of the other families who are part of the Frozen Olympics any lessons in dogsledding?" Herb asked. He'd seen some of the other families working to decorate their family sleds in the private stalls inside the dogsledding kennels, and he'd noticed that a few of them had gone out on rides where they were inside the sled compartment with other mushers driving. But he knew no one else had spent quite as much time as he had in the kennel building and yard since they'd arrived. "Has anyone else gotten a sneak peek at the route?"

"A few have gone out for guided trail rides with the dogs, so they could learn some basic skills," Philip said, nodding. "And we'll offer everyone a quick refresher course that morning, so all the groups understand how to work a sled and aren't forced into the race without feeling comfortable. But you will definitely have an advantage, because you've spent so much time getting to know the dogs and the sport. You're a natural, and I hope that means you'll win the final race."

Herb hoped that, too. What if they *did* win? What if they were declared the Frozen Best? Herb was already pretty sure they *were* the best family of all, but winning an ice castle of their very own at the B&B and being crowned champions sure would feel good. And if Herb could be a big part of helping them win the final event, that would feel even better!

Suddenly, Philip pointed to a herd of reindeer racing across a snowy hill not too far off. Herb had seen reindeer milling around in one of the large, fenced yards near the Icehotel, but he'd never seen anything like this in nature, in the real world. The way the slanted sunlight glinted on the sparkling snow beneath their hooves made it look—for a moment—as if they'd lifted off into the air and were soaring through space like the crew that pulled Santa's sleigh. With Philip the Santa-look-alike standing beside him, Herb suddenly imagined what it would feel like to fly through the sky like that with the *real* Santa Claus, pulled by a team of reindeer. He closed his eyes as he held tight to the handle of the sled and let the wind whip at his face as his team of strong, powerful sled dogs pulled him across the snow-covered Arctic.

What if my sled took flight? he briefly wondered. Then he opened his eyes and let the happy *what-if* sink in and take over his thoughts, letting all his worries fall out of the back of the sled as they sailed across the snow toward the Icehotel, back toward Herb's family.

From the Sketchbook of Freddy Peach:

ICEHOTEL SLED DOG SPECTACULAR

STARRING:

Owl

Oops

Old Man

Bongo

Grinch

Pickle Jim

Ontario

Big Mama Suzanne

Peepers

Gary

Tootsie

Terri

Terry

Pablo

PeeWee

Gitchi

15

* * * * * * * * * * * * * * * * *

A FROZEN PECK OF PEACHES

Okay, so maybe Lucy had gotten a little carried away with the whole ice-carving thing. She was usually a little less *sneaky*, but there was something about these Frozen Olympics—and Ellen Proetz, specifically—that was bringing out a competitive streak Lucy had never realized she had.

Shortly after Lucy and Freddy had arrived in the ice-carving studio on the third day of their trip, one of the dads from Washington, as well as the mother-daughter team from Maine, had all swung by for a quick session to prep for the Frozen Olympics ice-carving contest the next day. After the group lesson, Lucy pretended to leave and head out with everyone else. She wanted to throw Ellen Proetz off her case. But as soon as she was out of sight of the other sweepstakes winners, Lucy had doubled back toward the ice-carving studio to spend more time working on her newfound skills. She wanted to complete at least one perfect ice peach before the next day's competition, just to know she could do it before she was carving under pressure.

By the time she felt confident that she was ready for the second-to-last event in the Frozen Olympics, it was nearly dark outside. Freddy had left when everyone else did, hoping to spend some time working with Herb on their family dogsled decorations in the kennel. Lucy knew the "amazing" Proetz family, the mother-daughter team from Maine, and the two dads and twins had headed over to work on personalizing their family sleds as well. She assumed the Banerjee family from Michigan was probably already over there. All five teams had been given some basic tools and props to decorate their sleds for the final Frozen Olympics race, and each was assigned a stall in the kennel yard, where they could work on their family's design in private, so none of the other competitors could see what they were doing. Lucy was desperate to get a peek at what other people were planning, and maybe even "accidentally" knock a few decorations off the Proetz family's sled, but she knew both of those things would be crossing a line she wasn't willing to cross.

Luckily, she trusted both of her brothers to make good headway on their dogsled decorations, which meant her time was better spent preparing for the second-to-last competition instead. As she left the ice-carving studio, Lucy's stomach rumbled, and she realized it was probably just about time for dinner. Her dad should be getting back from his work trip any minute now—in fact, since it was just about dark, the scientist team was probably already home—and all five Peaches had made plans to eat dinner together before heading over to watch Freddy's theatrical debut.

Lucy walked across the snowy Icehotel grounds toward the warm hotel, eager to see her dad and looking forward to watching her brother fight onstage that night. She peeled off her snowsuit in the equipment room, hung it up, and hustled inside. But when Lucy got to the restaurant, she found her two brothers and Great Aunt Lucinda alone at their family's table, with two empty chairs—one for her, one for her dad.

"Where's Dad?" Lucy asked, pulling her staticky hair back into a messy ponytail.

Herb and Freddy both shrugged. Lucy could tell her youngest brother was worried. He always chewed his lower lip when he was anxious about something.

"I thought he said they would be back by dark

tonight," Freddy said, obviously not noticing that Herb was already fretting and didn't need to be reminded that their dad was late.

"I'm sure they just got caught up with their project and lost track of time," Great Aunt Lucinda said reassuringly. "They'll certainly be home soon." Dinner arrived then, and the topic shifted to the day's activities, but throughout the meal Lucy could see Herb constantly looking over his shoulder to see if Dad would suddenly appear. They finished dessert—every single one of them chose the gooey chocolate-mud-cake-brownie thing with fresh whipped cream on top—and even at the end of the meal, Dad still wasn't back.

"I don't want to perform in the show tonight if Dad's not here to see it," Freddy said, sounding a little desperate. "I'm gonna go over to the theater and tell Anna I might have to wait until tomorrow night to take my turn onstage."

"I'm sure—" Lucy began to say that she was sure their dad would be back by the time the performance started that night, but the truth was, she *wasn't* sure. Yes, Dad had proven to be reliable for the past eight or nine months or so, but before that, he'd flaked out a lot. He'd promised them he'd be home from the research station tonight, but maybe something had come up and Dad had chosen to stay and work instead of coming back to them when he'd promised. "Yeah," Lucy said, shifting. "It might be a good idea to see if you can perform tomorrow night instead."

Obviously bummed, Freddy schlumped away from the table and headed out into the cold and blowing snow to tell his fellow actors that he needed to wait a night to make his big stage debut. Meanwhile, Great Aunt Lucinda ordered herself a second cup of decaf coffee. As the restaurant emptied out, and still Dad did not show, Lucy began to grow frustrated. She knew how much Herb wanted to trust their dad—Lucy did, too, but not as desperately and trustingly as Herb—and she hated that he was letting them down. Again. He'd promised to be back in time for Freddy's performance; he'd promised to be back in time for the ice-carving contest; he'd promised his work trip would only take him away from their family adventure for one night.

"Do you think he could be hurt?" Herb asked softly.

"No," Great Aunt Lucinda said, patting him on the hand. "I'm sure something important came up, and they just decided to wait until tomorrow to come back."

❦ ❦ ❦

The next morning, after another partially sleepless night in the Icehotel, when Lucy was heading back inside to the warm hotel from her third night in a row sleeping on a bed of ice, she bumped into a woman she recognized as one of the researchers Dad had been talking with on the first day. "Hi!" Lucy said, holding up a mittened hand. "I'm Lucy, Walter Peach's daughter."

"Yes, of course," the woman said, nodding. "Thanks again for letting him join us on our expedition."

Lucy released a relieved sigh. "You were part of the group that went up to the research station with him, right? When did you get back?"

"Actually, Katia and I had to come back on the snowmobile early yesterday morning. She began to feel awful just after we arrived at the station—she thinks she ate something that made her sick before we went north—so the two of us returned almost as soon as we got there," the woman said. "But Johan and Walter stayed behind to finish up the project."

"I thought they were supposed to come back last night," Lucy said, her stomach dropping. "My dad said he'd only be gone one night."

The woman waved her off with a smile. "You know scientists," she said, chuckling. "Once they get caught up in their research, the world drops away. Without the two of us there to help, I'm guessing the project took a little longer than planned. They'll surely be back soon."

Lucy didn't like this excuse and explanation. Science could be used as a reasonable explanation for many things—a reason to get important vaccines that might help save lives or climate change, for example—but science *wasn't* a legitimate excuse for going back on your word to your kids. She thought her dad had realized that by now. She was angry with Dad for making yet another promise, and then not keeping it.

When Dad *still* wasn't back by the time the ice-carving competition started, Herb was practically spinning with worry. Lucy was able to put her mind off her annoyance and mild concern by focusing on her ice-carving project, but she could tell Herb wasn't as easily distracted. Even when Lucy managed to *win* the whole ice-carving competition with her nearly perfect peck of frozen peaches, Herb barely even celebrated the win with his family. He just stared off into the distance and kept waiting for Dad to appear on the horizon.

But no matter how hard Herb stared, and how hard Lucy wished for him to show up, Dad didn't come. With each minute of the morning that ticked by, Lucy's faith and trust in the dad she'd finally begun to believe in again slipped further and further away.

FROZEN OLYMPICS
SCORE SHEET
· · · · · · · · · · ·

(totals going into the final dogsledding race!)

Proetz Family Farm (Montana): 3 3 5 6

Seaside B&B (Washington): 2 3 3 3

Anderson's Resort (Michigan): 1 1 4 4

Cottages in the Middle of Nowhere (Maine): 0 3 3 5

Peachtree B&B (Minnesota): 0 2 3 6

16

⭐ ⭐ ⭐ ⭐ ⭐ ⭐ ⭐ ⭐ ⭐ ⭐ ⭐ ⭐ ⭐ ⭐

THE DAD PROBLEM

After Lucy's big ice-carving contest win for the family, Freddy brought her and Great Aunt Lucinda to the kennel to show them the progress he and Herb had already made on their sled decorations for the final Frozen Olympics race the next afternoon. Freddy had painted the old prop eggs he'd found at the Frozen Globe so they looked like beautiful, ripe peaches, and Lucy had brought her *frozen* peaches over from the ice-carving studio to repurpose as part of their decorations on the very back of the sled. Herb and Freddy had also begun to assemble a metal pie pan sort of thing that they planned to wrap around the sides of their dogsled. "Once we have the pie pan structure built and attached, we can cover this ugly metal with some of the wicker so it looks like our giant peach pie is nestled in a little basket. So charming, just like The Peachtree B and B."

"This is incredible," Great Aunt Lucinda said. "Is there something I can do to help?"

"How are your sewing skills?" Freddy asked.

"Barely passable," Great Aunt Lucinda said with a laugh. "But I've got time to figure it out and can probably ask the older gentleman from the Michigan family to help if I need it. I've seen him knitting in the lobby quite a bit this week."

Freddy nodded. "Okay, how would you feel about trying to sew some hats that look like peaches for each of us? You could stitch them and stuff them, or knit them, or whatever method you think is best. We basically need peach-shaped wigs, and you, Great Aunt Lucinda, are the best person for the job."

"You all want to wear *peach hats* during the race?" Great Aunt Lucinda exclaimed. "That is about the cutest thing I've ever heard in my life."

"We need to look like we're part of the pie when we're riding. Like we're a peck of Peaches baked inside," Freddy explained. "This dogsled design is going to be epic."

Great Aunt Lucinda set off, back to the warm hotel

lobby with her sewing instructions, while Freddy and his siblings continued to work on their sled decorations in the chill of the kennel yard. Nearby, other teams were working on their own sled decorations and Freddy could hear the chatter and clatter of art-in-progress. It was a sound he loved. Glancing over at his brother from time to time, Freddy could tell Herb was worried about their dad. But both he and Lucy were trying to keep their brother's mind off it by keeping him busy decorating and building. Art could be a great distraction.

However, if he was being honest, Freddy was now getting a little worried about their dad, too. For most of his life, Freddy had thought he and his dad were about as different as two people could be. Freddy liked art and random, *fun* facts, while Dad liked science and boring, *proven* facts.

But recently, Freddy had begun to realize that he and his dad had more in common than he had originally thought. They were both very passionate about the things they loved and tended to get caught up in and overcommitted to projects they were working on. Freddy admired his dad, because he obviously loved the work he did, but he also respected him for how he'd been working so hard to figure out how to do a better job of balancing time with their family and the time he spent at work. This wasn't like the Dad they'd all come to know over the past nine months or so, to make a promise he wasn't prepared to keep.

But maybe they'd all been wrong to assume that their last few Great Peach Experiments had brought their family closer together. Working as a team in the Peach Pie Truck had been fun, and helping to fix up the Peach Pit had been a lot of hard work. Maybe Dad was sick of spending so much time with his family, and he was planning to start shifting more of his time back to work?

By the time lunch rolled around, the three Peach kids had made a ton of progress on their sled and Freddy thought it *totally* looked like a pie, but none of them were having any fun anymore. It was clear that everyone was bummed Dad *still* hadn't returned from his trip. He was now nearly a full day late, and there was no sign of him nor any word from the research station.

"Can we *call* the research station or something?" Lucy blurted out of the blue, as she wrapped a shabby chunk of wicker around a piece of bendy metal. "There's got to be some way to get ahold of them and find out why they're not back yet, and get a sense of when they *are* planning to show up."

"I already checked," Herb said. "There isn't a phone or cell phone service at the research station. It's in the middle of nowhere."

"Did you know that the northeastern corner of Montana officially holds the title of 'Middle of Nowhere, USA'?" Freddy asked, hoping a random fact might help them all relax a bit. "But I'm guessing this research station is even *more* middle of nowhere than that corner of Montana, wouldn't you think?"

Lucy glared at him, just as Herb began to cry.

Suddenly, Philip popped his head around the corner of their sled-decorating area to say hello. When he noticed Herb was crying, he stepped back out and returned a minute or so later with one of the sleepy sled dog puppies nestled in his arms. He passed the pup to Herb, who buried his face in the dog's thick fur and continued to sob. "What's going on?" Philip asked gently.

"Our dad was supposed to be back yesterday afternoon from his trip up to some sort of research station way out in the middle of nowhere," Freddy began.

"But he's still not back and I want him back," Herb blubbered.

Philip nodded. "Ah, yes, I know this research station. The scientists always borrow a team of my dogs to get up there. Your dad must be with Johan. You need not worry; Johan is very smart and capable. I'm sure they're just fine, and that they'll return to the Icehotel very soon."

"He *promised*," Herb said, loudly enough that he woke the puppy, who'd been sound asleep in his arms. The puppy gazed up at Herb and slurped its wet tongue over Herb's running nose. Freddy cringed. He wasn't sure which was germier: a puppy's slobbery tongue, or Herb's slimy boogers. "Dad doesn't make promises and break them. He *doesn't*."

Freddy glanced at Lucy, and they shared a look. Herb was more willing to forgive their dad for the years after their mom died, when Dad had just sort of disappeared and forgotten how to be a father. But Freddy and Lucy weren't as quick to forgive and forget. Freddy *wanted* to believe that his dad was trustworthy and reliable now, but he didn't share Herb's never-ending hopefulness.

Lucy explained to Philip that two members of the research team had come back early on the snowmobile the previous morning, and now it was just Dad and one other scientist—this Johan guy, apparently—up at the research station along with the team of dogs. "It's just two of them, alone. We really don't need to worry, though, right?" She glanced at Herb, obviously hoping Philip would give the answer Herb needed to hear.

"Going up there with a team of two is not uncommon," Philip said. "No one would ever venture up there alone, especially in the winter, because it's so remote. But a team of two should be just fine."

"What if someone got hurt?" Herb asked.

"I'm sure no one is hurt," Lucy said, but Freddy thought she sounded less than sure.

"Even if something *did* happen to one of them," Philip said, "they each have a partner who can help get them back."

Freddy suddenly realized something. "But the only way they have to get back is by driving a sled dog team, right?"

Lucy nodded. "The two women came back together on the snowmobile yesterday morning. They left Dad and Johan up there with just the dogs and a sled."

"So, let's say for argument purposes," Freddy began, "something happened to the guy who knows how to drive a sled dog team. And *Dad* is his partner who needs to figure stuff out. How are they going to get back, then? Dad can't harness dogs or drive a dogsled. Even if he thinks he can figure it out, we all know he probably can't."

"Lucy is right," Philip said suddenly. "It's very unlikely that someone would have gotten hurt. I'm sure they're just caught up in their project and are coming back later than they planned. It happens to me all the time when I'm having a good time on a trip."

"It's not just later than they *planned*," Herb blurted out, still blubbering. "It's later than Dad *promised*. He *promised*, and you don't break promises."

"So, what do you want to do?" Freddy said, feeling helpless while also feeling very bad for his brother. "Drive up there and check on him?"

Herb's face suddenly brightened. "Yes," he said. "That's exactly what I want to do."

"You want to . . ." Lucy began, "go to the research station? The one in the middle of nowhere?"

"Can we?" Herb said, turning to Philip. "Can we ride up there and make sure everything and everyone is okay? He promised he'd be home by now." Freddy and Lucy looked at each other again, neither wanting to tell Herb what he really ought to have figured out on his own already: Dad's promises were a little like fool's gold. They looked and felt real on the surface, but when it was time to cash them in, they were worth nothing.

Philip looked unconvinced. "The research center is well over an hour away by sled, and it's going to be dark in not too long. We'd be cutting it close. I think you're better off waiting until tomorrow morning. By then, I'm sure he'll be back."

Herb shook his head vigorously, causing the pup to squirm right out of his arms. It scampered out into the snowy yard to romp with some of the other puppies. "Tomorrow will be too late. They need us now. I just know it." He turned to Freddy. "There's no way Dad would *choose* to miss the chance to see you perform onstage, right?"

Freddy shrugged. He'd hoped that was the case, but when Dad hadn't returned from his work trip the previous night, he had started to wonder.

"When he finds out he missed you *winning* the ice-carving competition," Herb said to Lucy, "Dad's going to be really sad."

Lucy blinked. Freddy knew his sister was disappointed their dad hadn't been there to see her carving skills at work. Lucy had serious talent!

"And there's no *way* he'd want to miss the final event

of the Frozen Olympics. That's how I know something must be wrong," Herb said. "It's our *family* dogsledding race. Dad *has* to be here for it. He's part of this family, and I don't want to win without him either in the sled or cheering us on at the finish line!"

Philip sighed. "I have a team of dogs all harnessed up and ready to roll," he said slowly. "If you really think we ought to check on him and his research partner, I could probably be convinced to drive a team up there. It's a beautiful day for a ride. I'd just need you to check with your aunt, to make sure she's okay with the idea. And if she's willing to let you make the trip, we would need to head out as soon as possible."

Freddy knew Great Aunt Lucinda would be okay with the idea. She was always willing to support people's passions; that's one of the things he loved most about her. In fact, if Great Aunt Lucinda hadn't been so supportive of Mom's passion for one day opening a B&B, Freddy's family never would have gotten to live in the Peach Pit! "Would we *all* go along?" Freddy asked. "Because I think if any one of us is going to go check on Dad, we should all go. We're better together, right? And then no one is stuck here, wondering and waiting to find out what's going on."

"If you're willing to cram in," Philip said, "I can fit all three of you in the sled. Herb can help me drive, and the two of you are about the same weight as a big load of gear."

Freddy looked at Lucy, who nodded her agreement. Then Lucy looked to Herb, who was already vigorously nodding. "Let's get Great Aunt Lucinda's permission," Freddy told his siblings. "And then squeeze these three Peaches into a sled. To the middle of nowhere we go!"

17

IN SEARCH OF SCIENTISTS

Herb couldn't quite believe he had convinced Philip and his siblings to venture north to check on Dad, but he just *knew* something must be very, very wrong. He *trusted* Dad. Herb was certain that if their dad had told them he would be home by the previous night, he should have been home by last night; the fact that he wasn't raised Herb's worry *what-if* alarm.

The rest of his family kept claiming Dad had probably just gotten caught up in work, so Herb had assumed they would all continue to dismiss his concerns and tell him to go have a cup of hot chocolate or something to get his mind off his worries. But after explaining himself as carefully as he could, his siblings had actually *listened* to him, and now he and Philip were standing side by side, driving a dogsled north together, with Freddy and

Lucy squeezed into the riding compartment in front of them.

Today was the coldest day of their trip to Sweden so far, but Herb barely noticed the wind biting at his face as they soared north, through the snow, in their sled. All he could think about was Dad, and how he hoped he really was okay and that nothing was wrong. Philip had assured Herb that there was only one safe and clear route they could take to get to the research station, which sat at the foot of a massive glacier, and if Dad and Johan left the station to come home while their rescue team was heading north to find them, they would undoubtedly pass each other along the way.

As the minutes of their journey flew by, Herb hoped that's what would happen; that they would see a line of dogs emerge through the stark white line of the horizon, and as they drew near, Dad would be standing beside Johan on the back of the sled. But the trail ahead remained clear, and there was no sign of dog or sled tracks having passed through this way since the previous afternoon's snowfall. With each mile they covered, heading north toward the research station set at the base of the glacier, Herb grew more and more concerned. Part of him knew his siblings and Great Aunt Lucinda and everyone else was probably right; that Dad had maybe just gotten caught up in his work and hadn't realized (or cared) that by not coming back when he promised he would, it would cause Herb to worry. But an even bigger part of Herb believed that Dad wouldn't do that; that there must be something very, very wrong to force their dad to break a promise he'd made.

Herb had always wished there was something more he could have done to save Mom when she'd been sick with cancer; if Dad needed him now, Herb would never forgive himself if he didn't do everything he could to try to help.

Their sled went so fast—and their faces were so covered in warm layers to protect their skin from the frozen air—that it was impossible to talk during the journey. Herb glanced over the front of the sled and saw that Freddy and Lucy were curled up under a blanket, huddled together, their heads and bodies completely hidden under the thick fabric. It reminded Herb of the blanket forts they used to make with Mom, in their old house's living room. The forts were always lumpy and filled with holes where the daylight from outside the blanket-tent could peek through, but Mom always managed to create a cozy, snuggly spot in the very middle of everything that fit the four of them and felt like a little bear den. She would drag piles of picture books inside their secret space and read to them using the dim light from an old headlamp that she wore over her mass of fluffy hair.

Herb was so caught up in his memories that he didn't notice a line of little huts that suddenly dotted the horizon ahead. They'd been riding through blank nothingness for so long that it was strange to suddenly see several small red buildings sticking out of the snow at the base of a jagged mountain covered in a sheet of snow. The huts reminded him of the little red hotels you could buy to put on your squares in the game of Monopoly. "Just there," Philip said, pointing to the huts as he nudged Herb in the ticklish part of his side. "That's the research station."

The station was much larger than Herb had been expecting. It was also very *different* from what Herb had been picturing. He'd been expecting one small, steely, harsh-looking building perched atop a crusty chunk of ice on a mountainside. But this was like a very, *very* small town, with six or seven cozy-looking cabins scattered here and there in a fold at the base of the mountain, looking as if they'd been dropped out of the sky and left to stand where they landed.

Herb instructed his team of dogs to stop outside the nearest cabin. Philip put a big hook in the ground and tied the team to a tree so they couldn't take off without them. But the dogs looked exhausted, so Herb guessed they might be grateful for the rest. Many of the dogs immediately plunked down in the snow, panting after their long, hard run.

Lucy, Freddy, and Herb popped off the sled and followed Philip through the small village, searching for signs of their dad and Johan and the dogsledding team. Suddenly, Herb heard the faint, familiar sound of dogs barking from inside a building on the farthest end of the complex. He ran toward the sound, careened around a corner, and found a few sled dogs milling about in a small, fenced, snowy yard. Herb could see that there was a large doggie door that allowed them to pass from inside to outside whenever they liked. He raced around the corner, searching for a human door to enter through. The rest of the pack was inside the building, but there were no people to be seen. "This is the kennel," Herb told the others, pushing his way back outside. "But no Dad, just dogs."

The dogs barked and yipped, begging Herb to return to play with them. Much as Herb wanted to sit and give them all ear rubs and kisses, he needed to find his dad. The fact that the pack of dogs was still here at the research center meant Dad and Johan hadn't left yet. Which meant they weren't lost, or stranded without transport, or any of the other logical things that might have caused their dad to break his promise.

The group continued their search, poking their heads into several of the small cabins, but finding no sign of life. Finally, they came to the second-to-last cabin, and Herb noticed something that gave him hope: footprints in the snow near the door!

Herb raced inside, more eager than ever to see his dad, but when he stepped through onto the rough mat inside the door of this cabin, there was just an empty room. It was warmer than the other huts had been, and Herb was pretty sure he could smell Dad's favorite flavor of tea. But maybe that was just wishful thinking.

Herb spun around, looking helplessly at his siblings. "He's not here," he said. "Where could they be?"

"They must be out on the glacier," Philip said. "That's where they do a lot of their research projects." He gave Herb a sad smile and said, "It seems maybe folks were right when they suggested your dad and Johan got caught up with the project they're out here working on. Everything seems just fine. . . ."

Herb sighed. It did seem that way. He'd been so sure of his dad's ability to keep a promise. He didn't want to admit that everyone else was right. Lucy wrapped her arm around him, but Herb shrugged her off and pushed the door open to head back outside and figure out their next move.

Suddenly, he crashed into someone. "Dad!" Herb exclaimed, wrapping his arms around his dad's giant snowsuit.

"Herb?" Dad said, quickly hugging him back. He looked startled as he stammered, "Oh, Herb, thank God. What are you . . . how . . . I don't—"

"You're late," Herb announced, his voice muffled by Dad's snowsuit. "You were supposed to be back at the Icehotel yesterday."

"Oh, Herbie, I'm so sorry. How did you get up here? Are you alo—" Just then, Lucy, Freddy, and Philip stepped out the door of the little research cabin.

Herb glanced at his siblings, noticing that neither of them was racing forward to give their dad a hug. He could tell they were both still angry with Dad for breaking his promise. Suddenly, Herb backed up slightly. Dad seemed absolutely, perfectly fine—just surprised, the way he sometimes did when Herb interrupted him while he was reading an article or working at his laptop. Maybe there *wasn't* a good excuse for him being late. "Why didn't you come back when you said you would?"

"It's such a relief to see you!" Dad exclaimed, not answering the question. "Are you all wearing warm clothes? I—"

Lucy snorted. "We just rode in a sled, miles out into the middle of nowhere, to come check on you. Of *course* we're wearing warm clothes. We're not stupid."

"Please, come with me," Dad said, quickly ushering them away from the cabin. "Hurry. I don't know how or why you decided to come up here, but it's a very good thing you did. We need help. Badly."

Herb followed his dad, who was now practically running. He led the four of them away from the research station, up the side of the mountain onto a massive slab of icy snow that Herb guessed must be the glacier. "Watch your step," Dad said, turning back to warn his kids. "Follow exactly behind me, and don't step out of line." Herb wasn't sure what it was about his dad's voice, but something in his tone told Herb—and everyone else—that they should follow his instructions and do as they were told.

They continued to climb upward, carefully following their dad's trail in a line of Dad-Herb-Freddy-Lucy-Philip. Dad's pace slowed just as Herb noticed a long, thin crack in the glacier up ahead of them. There was a sled next to it, along with all kinds of ropes and piles of gear and tools set up in heaps alongside the crack. "What's that?" he asked, pointing.

"A crevasse," Freddy blurted out knowingly. "It's a deep crack that forms between two sheets of glacial ice."

"That's exactly what it is," Dad confirmed, suddenly coming to a stop. Herb moved right up next to his dad and looked down into the crack. And that's when he spotted Johan—the other scientist who'd been out there working with Dad—twenty feet down inside that sheet of ice.

18

A CRACK IN THE ICE

Lucy gasped. "Is he okay?" She looked down and could see the scientist was perched on a very small ice ledge inside the crevasse. The crack in the ice wasn't super-wide, and it narrowed quite quickly below him. The ledge seemed to be holding Johan from slipping farther, but it did seem—to Lucy, anyway—that if he fell any farther he'd be squeezed in enough to keep him from sliding down-down-down into the blue-black noth-ingness at the bottom of the crevasse. That's what she *hoped*, but Lucy *knew* a grand total of nothing about gla-cial crevasses.

Johan waved one arm feebly from below. "I've been better," he groaned, wincing as he spoke. He was wrapped in tons of blankets, with several hats stuffed onto his head. There was a rope that snaked down from the edge of the crevasse to where Johan stood, hovering on that little lip of ice below.

"We think he may have broken his arm in the fall," Dad said. "I've been trying—and failing—to pull him up on my own. Thank goodness you came when you did, since I don't know if he could have survived another night in there. And I couldn't get back on my own to get help, and—" Dad's voice cut off, the sound of desperation and fear choking his words.

Lucy spun around and saw that Philip was already working on tying a whole collection of ropes and clasps into special knots that looked like a makeshift sled dog harness. "How long has he been down there?"

"Since yesterday afternoon," Dad began. "Just as we were on our way back to the station to pack up and head home, Johan slipped. He was in the lead and didn't see the crack in time to stop himself from sliding in. Normally, you can see these glacial crevasses and either avoid them altogether or they're narrow enough to step over. But this one was covered with fresh snow, and Johan fell into it."

"It could be worse," Johan called up softly from below. "I could easily have fallen fifty or a hundred feet, or this crevasse could have been filled with icy water at the bottom, in which case I would have frozen to death within an hour or so. As it is, I'm dry and not so far down that you can't help get me out."

As far as silver linings went, Lucy didn't really think this one was very impressive. He had a possibly broken arm, was standing twenty feet down inside a glacier, and it was well below freezing outside. "Have you been trying to pull him out since yesterday afternoon?" Lucy asked, as Dad helped Philip lower the rope down to Johan. She couldn't believe Herb had been right—Dad *hadn't* broken his promise. He'd been in trouble, and if it hadn't been for Herb, no help would have come.

"We didn't have anything useful with us when he fell," Dad explained. "I ran back to the station to get a sled with some ropes and more warm clothes for him, then we tried to figure out what we were going to do." He explained that he and Johan had worked together to try to get him out by pulling him up, but Johan's wounded arm kept him from being able to hold his end of the rope, and Dad wasn't strong enough to hoist him out on his own.

"Then it got dark," Dad went on. "So, I ran back and got us warm soup and tea and brought a lamp and more blankets up here so I could keep him company overnight. There was nothing we could do in the dark except talk and try to figure out what our plan would

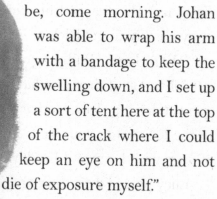

be, come morning. Johan was able to wrap his arm with a bandage to keep the swelling down, and I set up a sort of tent here at the top of the crack where I could keep an eye on him and not die of exposure myself."

Lucy gawped at her dad. How had he known to do all those things? Suddenly, she felt *very* bad for assuming the worst about her dad when he hadn't come back when he'd said he would. He'd let them down in order to try to save his friend. "But—" Lucy began. "But he's still down there."

Dad cringed. "This morning, when it was clear I wasn't going to be able to drag him out on my own, we realized I needed to try to get back to town to bring help. I've been trying to get the dogs and sled ready to go, but I couldn't work the harnesses and I was worried about driving them anywhere on my own." Dad turned and looked at Lucy and her brothers, shaking his head as if he couldn't quite believe his eyes. "I don't know how to drive a sled, and I didn't know the way—" He cut off, his voice full of emotion. "But now you're here. You saved us." He wrapped his kids in his arms, but broke away quickly to get back to helping Johan.

"We're here," Philip agreed. "And luckily, once we get Johan out of there, we have two people who are very good at driving sleds. Herb can take you and Johan back to the Icehotel in your sled, and I'll lead the other pack of dogs with Lucy and Freddy."

Lucy peered over the edge of the crevasse, watching as Johan stepped into Philip's rope harness. He double-checked the knots and wrapped his good arm around the rope pulley. Dad and Philip each grabbed the rope, then gestured for the kids to hold on as well. "Kids in the middle," Philip said. "We don't need anyone else sliding into the crevasse." Philip stood at the front, then Lucy, Freddy, and Herb, with Dad at the back. "On three, we all pull. Slow, but steady," Philip said, acting like he'd dragged people out of glaciers plenty of times before. Suddenly, she wondered if he *had*, and made a note to ask him. Later. "Try not to ease up, so he doesn't slide back down again."

"It's like a life-or-death version of tug o' war," Freddy said helpfully, as they all began to pull.

"One," Philip said. Then he called out, "Johan— ready, *ja*?"

"*Ja!*" Johan said, calling out his agreement.

"Two," Philip said. Lucy wrapped the rope around her mittened hand, not caring if it dug into her skin. They had to get him out of there! "Three."

Slowly but steadily, they all pulled. Lucy took a small step back and noticed that the rope was moving—inch by inch—out of the ice crack. She could suddenly feel Johan's full weight tug on the rope as he was lifted off the ledge he'd been stuck on below. She grunted and dug her feet into the snow, trying to make sure she didn't slip and lose her hold.

"I'm halfway up," Johan called out. "Please hurry."

"We've got this," Lucy said aloud, as much to reassure herself as everyone else.

They continued to pull, taking teeny steps back in the snow with each inch of the rope that emerged from the depths of the crevasse. When they'd gone back about fifteen feet or so, Philip said, "Can you Peaches hold the rope while I try to grab him and pull him the rest of the way up?"

"Yes," Lucy said, clenching her teeth.

"I'm letting go," Philip said. As soon as he said it, the rope slipped just a little. Lucy let out a squeak, but then she felt the rest of her family lean back and the rope was still and taut once again. Philip belly-crawled toward the edge of the crevasse and reached his arm down to grab at Johan's good arm. As soon as he had a hold on him, he called, "Walter, come help!"

The Peach kids continued to hold the rope taut as Dad and Philip pulled Johan up and over the ridge of the glacial crack. They didn't let go, not until Johan rolled onto his side, away from the edge of the glacier to safety. He lay in the snow, looking up at the sky, panting.

"You're okay," Philip assured him. Then he looked at the Peaches and said, "But we need to move if we're going to get back before dark. And we *must* get back tonight, to get him medical care."

They loaded Johan into the sled and covered him up with blankets. He'd begun to shiver. "Shivering *can* be a good thing," Freddy told everyone as he tucked the blankets around Johan's shoulders and legs. "It helps your body stay warm by forcing the muscles to contract. But shivering only works for a little while, since your muscles get tired, and it can also be a sign you're fighting an infection, so . . ."

"So, let's move," Johan said, his teeth still chattering.

Lucy and Freddy worked together to pull the sled with Johan in it back toward the research station, while Dad, Herb, and Philip carried the rest of the gear down the glacier. "What on earth made you come all the way out here?" Dad asked, shaking his head in wonder as they walked swiftly back to the waiting dogs and warm buildings.

"Herb convinced us," Lucy said simply. "He kept saying 'a promise is a promise,' and was convinced that if you said you'd be back yesterday, you would have come back yesterday. We didn't really believe him, but he insisted you might need help and he wouldn't let us say no." Lucy glanced over at her little brother and gave him a smile.

Herb smiled back. Then he asked, "Now aren't you glad I trusted Dad?"

From the Sketchbook of Freddy Peach:
B&B ADVERTISING IDEAS

NOW FEATURING
KNITTING CLUB
EVERY THURSDAY!!*

You could make . . .

A rope!

A dinosaur!

A lasso!

A scarf!

and many other things!!

*Need a job? We're hiring a Knitting Instructor! No pay offered, but we provide **FREE PIE!**

19

THE FINAL COUNTDOWN

During the sled ride back to the Icehotel, Freddy asked if he could stand on the back of the sled beside Philip, so he could learn a little more about guiding the dogs. Seeing his younger brother at the helm of the other sled was cool, for sure, and it made Freddy feel like he was missing out on something fun himself.

"I was thinking," Freddy said loudly, to ensure Philip could hear him over the wind and through all his layers of warm gear. "We could maybe offer dogsledding as an activity option at our B and B. I think our guests could be interested in trying it out."

"Where do you live?" Philip asked.

"We live in a place called Duluth, Minnesota," Freddy said. Then he explained their hometown's location the way he always did. "It's the city right on the far western tip of Lake Superior. We're so far north in the United States that some people ask if Duluth is actually in Canada."

"I know exactly where Duluth is," Philip said excitedly. "Herb never told me where your family lives. I did a year studying abroad when I was in high school. I lived with a family in Two Harbors, Minnesota!"

"No way," Freddy said. Two Harbors was just up the North Shore of Lake Superior from Duluth. Only about a half hour by car, and it was also the hometown of Betty's Pies, which was one of the pie shops they'd stopped at to do research before their summer in the Peach Pie Truck! "When you lived in Two Harbors, did you ever eat at—"

Philip cut in, and together they said, "Betty's Pies?"

Laughing, Freddy added another, "No way. This is crazy. You've had Betty's Pies? And you lived less than thirty miles from us?"

"I lived there long before you were born, though. Two Harbors is actually the place where I started dog-sledding," Philip told Freddy. "I grew up in Stockholm, right in the middle of the biggest city in Sweden, and it wasn't until I went to Minnesota that I discovered my love for outdoor adventures. The family I stayed with had relatives who owned a kennel, and they taught me

all about mushing. We used to run the dogs on trails back in the woods just about an hour north of your hometown."

"Any chance you know anyone who might want to partner with our B and B to offer dogsledding lessons for our guests?" Freddy asked, realizing this could be an amazing extra opportunity they could offer to people who came to stay with them.

"Absolutely," Philip said, handing Freddy the reins to the sled. "I'll send an email to my favorite family in Two Harbors and let them know you'll be in touch. I'm sure they have plenty of contacts for you, and most dog-sledding kennels are eager to share the sport with as many people as possible."

Freddy grinned; this was too exciting. He could hardly wait to tell the rest of his family that he'd driven the team of dogs, but even more importantly, he couldn't wait to share this new idea. Visiting The Peachtree B&B in winter could be positioned as a chance for guests to explore all kinds of new-to-them outdoor activities! They could offer theme weekends, maybe. A few weekends of the winter could focus on dogsledding adventures along the North Shore. Other weekends would have a cooking theme, maybe, where they could teach people to bake pies in the Peach Pit's rustic kitchen. Maybe other week-ends they could offer ice-carving lessons . . . and butter carving in the spring and fall! The Minnesota State Fair was world-famous for showcasing butter sculptures, and surely the chance to learn such a strange art form in the butter-carving capital would be a draw for many visitors.

By the time they'd delivered Johan to the medical building in town, it was nearly dark outside. And when their sleds pulled into the kennel yard back at the Ice-hotel, Freddy knew it was already much too late for him to perform with the Frozen Globe's theater troupe that night. Besides, they had limited hours left in which to finish their sled design for the next day's final dogsledding race, and on top of that, Freddy was *starving*. He wondered if Anna and his castmates would be forgiving that he had missed two nights of performance in a row, but suspected once he told them the story of their family's glacial rescue, they would all understand. As far as Freddy was concerned, even if he *never* got his chance to perform onstage, this day's exciting events had more than made up for it.

Once they'd helped Philip unharness the dogs and put all the sleds and gear away, Freddy was practically faint with hunger. He was pretty sure he'd never gone this long without eating, and he was so desperate for dinner that he was almost tempted to dig his face into the vat of dog food and feast on the wet, sloppy mush with the sled dog team. Luckily, they finished up their chores before he had to resort to that.

With a quick wave and thanks to Philip for being a part of the day's rescue mission, Freddy and his family headed away from the kennel and toward the smell of food. They quickly dropped their wet, warm gear in the equipment room to dry, and just as Freddy began to wonder if he might evaporate from lack of food, they collapsed into their chairs at a table with Great Aunt

Lucinda in the warm hotel's dining room. While they devoured a meal of meatballs and mashed potatoes and lingonberry sauce and hot, salty gravy, each of the Peach kids took turns filling their great aunt in on their exciting afternoon.

"Well. I'll have you know, my day was just as exciting," Great Aunt Lucinda said after they'd finished their story, a twinkle in her eye.

"Really?" Herb asked.

"No," she said, laughing. "I had a nice, long sit in the sauna, made a batch of peach-shaped hats for your big race tomorrow, and whipped up some almond cookies in the hotel kitchen."

"That sounds so relaxing," Lucy said, closing her eyes and sinking deeper into her chair.

"You finished our hats?" Freddy asked, stifling a yawn.

"They're not going to win any prizes on *Project Runway*," Great Aunt Lucinda said, chuckling. "But I think they'll serve the purpose for which they're intended."

"I'm sure they're perfect," Freddy said. Then he looked around the table and said, "We can finish up the final touches on our sled in the morning, and we should be ready for the final event. But now the big question is:

Which of us is going to ride in the sled during the race, and who wants to watch and cheer?" Under the table, Freddy crossed his fingers, hoping he'd be chosen as one of the people who would get to ride in the sled for their final competition.

"I think the three of you kids should represent Team Peach," Dad said immediately. "Herb can drive the sled, and you and Lucy can be his teammates in the sled."

"But what about you, Dad?" Herb asked, looking slightly disappointed. "Don't you want to ride in the sled during the race, too?"

"I've had my share of excitement during this trip," Dad told them. "Frankly, I'd rather cheer—and you three certainly make a wonderful team."

"Are *you* okay not riding in the sled tomorrow?" Herb asked Great Aunt Lucinda.

She laughed and patted her long, elegant wig. "I'm more than okay with that plan."

"Then it's settled," Freddy declared. "Herb will drive, with me and Lucy in the sled for backup. We'll wear our peach hats—and carry swords?"

"No swords," Lucy, Herb, and Dad all said quickly together.

"One battle-ax?" Freddy suggested. "I can swing

it around to intimidate our competition?" He looked around the table for confirmation, but no one else seemed to be on board with the idea.

"Don't you think the peaches are enough?" Great Aunt Lucinda asked.

Freddy considered this for a minute. She was right: The Peaches *were* enough. More than enough.

"So . . . who wants to sleep in The Under the Sea Suite with me tonight?" He wiggled his eyebrows. No one said a word. "Only me? The rest of you are a big, fat no? Really?" Freddy shrugged, not entirely surprised.

After their dinner dishes were cleared away, the five Peaches sat in the hotel dining room together for nearly an hour, enjoying one another's company and talking about some of their favorite parts of the trip. It wasn't until halfway through his *second* dessert that Freddy realized his toes were *finally*, fully warm, and that's also when he realized he didn't really want to spend the night sleeping on ice all alone. Tonight, what he wanted more than anything, was to be together with his family, safe and warm and cozy. His people made him feel happy and loved—Freddy was so, so lucky to be part of such a wonderful family—and tonight, maybe *all* nights, *that* was more than enough for him.

20

THE FROZEN RACE

Herb stood at the back of his family's dogsled, surveying the sea of racers who surrounded them. It was almost time for the final event in the Icehotel's Frozen Olympics to start, and Herb couldn't wait to get going!

That morning, the Peach kids got to spend a little extra time putting finishing touches on their sled decorations, while all the other families who would be competing in the race had to get a quick, final tutorial on dogsledding and, for some, even learn the *basics* on how to guide their own team of dogs. Because Herb had spent most of his family's time in Sweden in the kennels and out on trails with Philip and his four-legged pack, he didn't need to do the refresher lesson—he was considered a true musher already!

After the lesson, the mother-daughter team from Maine had decided they didn't feel comfortable driving a sled on their own, so they asked to take one of the professional mushers along with them as a rider in their sled, just in case they needed some help along the way. When they realized that was an option, the Banerjee family from Michigan opted to do the same thing; which meant the grandparents would stay back to cheer while the dad and young son would work together to drive their sled, along with a helper from the kennels tucked into their sled's passenger compartment—just in case.

It turned out one of the two dads from the Washington family had taken several dogsledding lessons during the week, so he felt ready to drive their family's sled on his own, with his twin daughters nestled into a sleeping bag inside the sled. And though none of them had ever driven a sled on their own before, not one of the Proetz kids wanted to bring along a guide, since it would mean one of them would need to stay back and watch the race instead of riding; they insisted that they had learned enough in that morning's lesson to feel ready to race on their own. Herb knew Philip and some of his coworkers were planning to position themselves in a few tricky spots along the race route, just in case anyone got way off track or if any of the dogs needed to be rescued from their human team.

While Herb and his siblings waited for everyone else to harness and line up their teams and get ready at the start, Herb checked out some of the other families' sled designs. There was a wide variety of styles and themes represented in the five sleds, and they all looked great. But Herb could honestly say that their sled was the best of all.

Somehow, Freddy had managed to make it look like their sled was a rustic pie pan without making the sled bulky or heavy. Lucy and Freddy would squeeze together in the sled's passenger compartment, each wearing a stuffed peach hat. As soon as they were situated, Dad and Great Aunt Lucinda helped to nestle the big paper-mache peaches all around them in the sled, and Lucy's carved ice peaches were displayed carefully at the back of the sled, in special compartments on either side of Herb's feet. That morning, Freddy had drawn a big sign that read: THE PEACHTREE B&B: HOME OF GREAT AUNT LUCINDA'S FAMOUS PEACH PIE. It was perfect and tied everything together just so.

The mother-daughter sled from Maine was simple but cute. They'd built a pair of moose antlers out of sticks that the two women had mounted on either side of their sled. They were also wearing homemade moose antlers on their heads, and while Herb watched, he noticed that they were trying to affix tiny sets of plush antlers to each of the pups in their dogsledding team. The dogs were not cooperating.

The father-daughter sled from Washington was decorated to look like some sort of big fish. It wasn't the most professional-looking design Herb had ever seen, but based on the quality, Herb could tell that the dads had let the little daughters do a lot of the decorating and painting themselves, and that made him love that family's fish sled that much more.

The Banerjee family's sled had been decorated to look like a giant Christmas tree, complete with pine branches jutting out this way and that, a bunch of colorful paper ornaments

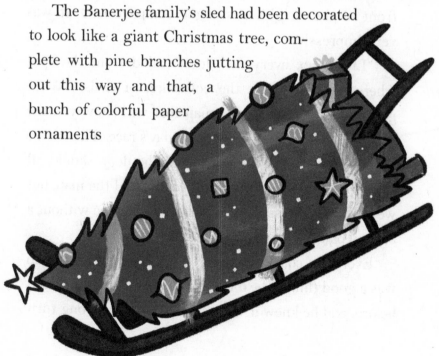

affixed to the branches, battery-powered lights, and a strand of sparkly garland wrapped around the whole thing. The professional musher who had to ride along with them in their sled was crammed into the only free space between a bunch of wrapped gifts that had also been stuffed inside the sled.

Ellen's family's sled had been completely covered in brown strips—made of wood, or paper, or Herb didn't know what—that made their sled look just like it was a tiny log cabin! There was a sign hanging from the back of the sled that said PROETZ FAMILY FARM, and they'd mounted a large, ice-carved pine tree in the front of the sleigh's passenger compartment. It was very impressive.

"Listen up, everyone!" Josef called from the spot where he stood near the collection of sleds. "We're going to give each team a map that will show you the route you're going to follow for today's race. The course is also very carefully marked and the dogs should all know the way, so I don't think you'll need the map, but we don't want to send you out into the Arctic without a backup plan!"

Everyone chuckled, but Herb knew having a map was a good thing—he'd taken a sled on part of this trail before, and he knew it was easier to make a wrong turn than some people might expect. He handed the map to his siblings, trusting that they could both help follow it and let Herb know if and when he needed to turn the dog team to stay on the course.

Josef continued. "We're going to stagger the start, so you're not all going out at the same time. Your final time will be calculated from when you cross the starting line until when you pass the finish line. We don't need to get any teams of dogs tangled at the start—that's not good for anyone. But there is a chance you could encounter another team on the course while you're out there. We just ask that, if you do come up on another team, you steer your sled around them on the left, to keep a safe distance from your competitors and their sled dog team. Let's make sure this adventure is safe and fun for all."

"We will have some staff members stationed out on the course, just in case," Philip added. "And you each have a walkie-talkie in your sled that should reach at least one of us, if you need help."

While the Icehotel staff checked everyone's walkie-talkies, and double-checked all the dogs' harnesses and lines, Herb stepped off the back of his family's sled and gave each dog in their team a little pep talk. "We're currently tied for first with the Proetz family," Herb whispered to Peewee, one of the lead dogs at the front of their line. "We *have* to beat them if we want to win." He glanced over at the Proetz kids and noticed that they were bickering over who would drive first and who would ride and study the map first.

"If we come in first out of everyone," Herb told Bob, Peewee's partner up front, "we win the Frozen Olympics. But if we *don't* win today, this could be anyone's game. Depending on what order we finish in, everyone still has a chance to take home the prize."

Herb had spent all of breakfast studying Lucy's sheet of paper where she'd kept track of everyone's points as they'd wrapped up each competition that week, and the leaderboard looked like this:

Proetz Family Farm (Montana): 6

Peachtree B&B (Minnesota): 6

Cottages in the Middle of Nowhere (Maine): 5

Anderson's Resort (Michigan): 4

Seaside B&B (Washington): 3

After doing the math, Herb knew the only way the Peaches were *guaranteed* to win the title of Frozen Best was if they won this sled dog race, and Herb liked guarantees. Any other outcome, and things got a little messier and less certain. If the Peaches didn't win today, their final position in the Frozen Olympics would depend on where everyone *else* finished in that day's race. Herb knew they didn't have any control over how all the other teams performed, but he did have control over *his* team. So, they just needed to win, it was that simple. That was the only sure thing.

The judges had drawn names to decide which order the teams would start in, and the mother-daughter team from Maine was the first to get sent out. They would be followed a few minutes later by the Banerjees' Christmas tree sled, then the father-daughter fish sled team, then the Proetz kids, and the Peaches would be last. "Last is good," Freddy assured his siblings. "Every time we pass another sled, we'll know we're that much closer to winning."

When it was finally their time to line up at the starting area, Herb gently guided his team of dogs right up to the front. Dad and Great Aunt Lucinda were standing there, cheering and clapping alongside the grandparents from Michigan, the other dad from Washington, and the Proetz kids' parents. It was pretty neat, Herb thought, that all the other teams were cheering for them even though they were all competing with one another for a prize and the title of Frozen Best.

As soon as Josef gave Herb the signal that it was time for them to start, Herb eased up on the sled's brake and gave his dogs the command to go: "All right!" Lucy and Freddy whooped from their cozy seat inside the sled and waved their homemade Peach hats in the air.

Because they were the last ones to start, it was very clear which way they needed to go. The route was mapped out for them with dog tracks and sled prints from all the teams that had set out before them. Herb felt safer with the map tucked inside the sled up front with Lucy and Freddy, but he could already tell they probably wouldn't need it. The course had been marked clearly enough that it would be almost impossible to get lost.

It still felt crazy, Herb thought, to be driving a sled and team of dogs through the snow all by himself. He was glad he'd had a chance to practice driving a sled the previous afternoon when they'd brought Johan—who was feeling much better now that his arm was wrapped up and he wasn't stuck inside a glacier—back from the research station. Yesterday, he'd had his dad standing by his side at the back of the sled, in order to give Johan room to stretch out in the sled; having Dad by his side had given Herb a little extra confidence. But today, his family was relying on him and him alone to stand at the back of the team and lead their sled to victory. He wanted to make them proud!

Up ahead, Herb could see the faintest outline of another team on the course in front of them. "Is that the Proetz kids' sled?" Freddy yelled out. "This is our first pass!"

Herb wasn't sure who it was. But as they drew closer, and Herb guided their team of dogs to the left so they could pass the other sled, he could see that it wasn't the Proetz kids; it was the father and his two daughters, who had started out third. As the Peaches slid past them, the dad and girls all turned and waved, and Herb could see that they were having a wonderful time. They weren't going fast, by any means, but none of them seemed to care that they weren't on track to win the race.

Herb assumed the fish sled must be going especially slowly since they'd passed it so quickly. But then, just a minute or two later, they passed the Banerjee family Christmas sled, and then less than a minute after that, they also passed the mother-daughter team and their cute moose antlers. Suddenly, Herb realized the Peach sled must actually be going quite *fast*, if they'd already passed three other teams who had started the race long before them.

The only team left in front of them now was the Proetz Family Farm sled, and Herb was determined to catch up. They were the only thing standing between the Peaches and victory. With a giant smile plastered onto his frozen face, Herb let out a whoop and a holler, just as Freddy shouted, "Peach power!"

Adjusting the cozy peach hat on top of his head, Herb dropped a pair of ski goggles over his eyes to block out the freezing air and focused his gaze on the snowy path ahead. As the dogs cut a swift and steady path through a narrow, tree-lined portion of the racecourse, Herb finally allowed himself to imagine the happy moment when his family would be crowned the Frozen Best.

21

STUCK IN THE SNOW

Lucy sat squeezed beside Freddy in their makeshift peach pie sled, trusting Herb to lead their family's team of dogs to victory. She couldn't believe how confident her little brother had gotten with his newfound dog-sledding hobby and hoped Herb would have a chance to continue to visit a kennel every so often when they returned to Minnesota. Herb had been thrilled to hear that Philip actually *knew* someone who worked at a kennel near Duluth—it was called White Wilderness Sled Dog Adventures, she was pretty sure—that he was planning to introduce them to. It would be so fun to be able to share this kind of activity with guests at The Peachtree B&B, too!

They'd already passed three other family dogsled teams. The only team still ahead of them was Ellen and the other Proetz kids, so Lucy had her eyes set on the snowy path, hoping to catch a glimpse of their only remaining competition. Since the Peach sled and the Proetz sled had started last and second to last, and both teams had now passed everyone else, it was obviously going to be one of these two sleds who would win the Frozen Olympics. The Peach and Proetz families were tied with the most points going into this final race, so whichever of them finished with the quickest time in the final race would be crowned the Frozen Best.

Josef had told all the competitors that any bonus points awarded for the best sled decorations would only be used to break a *tie*. The bonus points couldn't make one team slip out of first place if they'd won the most points during the week's main contests. So, the Peaches had to win this race. They *had* to. The Proetzes had started before them, so they didn't technically *need* to pass them in order to have the fastest time—but if they *did* pass them, it sure would make Lucy feel a whole lot less nervous. And it would make the Peaches the clear and obvious winners!

Just after they'd passed the other three sleds, the Peaches had glided past Anders, who'd been stationed at one of the most confusing turns in the race. They had waved and whooped, yelling hello as they zipped past.

They'd also flown past Lo, who was positioned at the far edge of the forested section. She was sitting astride a snowmobile and cheered as they sailed by. Now, out in a section of what seemed to be vast and never-ending whiteness, Herb guided their sled dog team past a bright red church that stood alone in the middle of the snow. Just on the other side of the church, Philip was waiting with another snowmobile and waved a hearty hello. "Are you doing okay, Peaches?" he called out.

"*Ja!*" Herb yelled back, which Lucy had by now figured out meant "yes" in Swedish. She'd also learned that though the word *sounded* like "yaw," it was spelled like it should be "jaw." Learning other languages was tricky! She could only imagine how hard it must have been for all these Swedes at the Icehotel to learn English, with all the funny rules her language had, like "*I* before *E* except after *C*" (unless it was a word like *beige* or *weight* or *caffeine*—so confusing!).

"You're nearly done with the race," Philip called to them. "This is the final checkpoint, but Herb, you should know the way back from here without any trouble. And I'm happy to report that the Proetz kids aren't that far ahead of you!"

Lucy took a deep breath and blew all the warm air out, instantly regretting it when her face covering iced up in front of her mouth. But knowing they weren't that far behind the only other team who could beat their time made her both nervous and excited. "Go, Herb!" she yelled out. "Go, dogs!"

"Don't just call them dogs!" Herb yelled back in what Lucy could tell was a peeved tone of voice. "Their names are Peewee, Bob, Big Mama Suzanne, Old Man, Terri with an *I*, and Terry with a *Y*." Lucy wasn't even going to *attempt* to remember and call out all those dog names. She didn't know how Herb could possibly keep them all straight, since most of the dogs looked so similar, and she knew he'd get even *more* frustrated if she said any of the names wrong.

Not long after they'd passed by Philip and the church, Lucy spotted a blot of darkness interrupting the bright white snow up ahead. "Is that another sled?" she asked Freddy, who was squeezed in beside her, huddled under their shared pile of blankets.

Freddy craned his neck, trying to see over the line of dogs out in front of them. From their low vantage point inside the sled's riding compartment, it was difficult to see straight ahead. "I think it might be!" Freddy exclaimed, bouncing a bit inside his seat. Lucy could hear barking dogs and howls up ahead; it had to be a team of sled dogs. It just *had* to be.

Their sled continued to glide closer and closer to the team in front of them. As they drew even nearer, Herb cried out, "It's them! We caught the Proetzes!"

Freddy and Lucy both let out squeals of excitement. Then, suddenly, Lucy had a vision of Ellen Proetz guiding *her* family's sled into the path of the Peach family sled. What if Ellen and her brothers had intentionally slowed down, just to try to *sabotage* them? Maybe they had plans to try to take the Peaches out as they passed, in order to eliminate their only remaining competition. "Come on, Herb," Lucy said loudly. "Give them lots of space and pass carefully!"

A moment later, as they pulled up on the left side of the Proetz sled, Lucy noticed that Ellen and her brothers were sitting atop a tipped-over sled. They weren't moving at all and didn't appear to be in any position to take the Peaches out . . . especially since their line of dogs seemed to be all tangled up in their harnesses and leads.

Herb guided the peach pie sled to a stop alongside the Proetz kids. "Whoa!" he called to his own team of dogs, who barked to greet their kennel mates from the other team.

"Herb!" Lucy said in a loud whisper. "What are you doing? Go!"

"Are you okay?" Herb called out to the Proetz family.

Lucy could answer that herself . . . their sled was tipped over and their dogs were in a big crowd of ropes and fur, rather than a tidy line that looked ready to run.

"Does it *look* like we're okay?" Ellen spat back. She kicked at the snow packed under her feet, then stood up from their family's toppled sled and began fussing with a few of the dogs' harnesses to try to untangle them. The dogs were having none of it; they backed away and jumped and yipped every time Ellen moved toward them to help. None of them seemed hurt, but they also weren't standing in any kind of organized order.

"Is anyone hurt?" Freddy asked. Lucy seriously hoped the Proetzes would say no, so the Peaches could just move on their merry way and win this thing.

"No," the oldest Proetz kid said. "We're not hurt, but we're pretty stuck. Our sled tipped, the dogs got spooked, and that led to a whole bunch of other problems. During the Sled Talk, the kennel guy told us if our sled tips, we're just supposed to sit on it and make sure the dogs don't take off without us. So, that's what we're doing."

"That's true," Herb said. "You should never let go of your sled. Do you want me to—"

"Did you walkie-talkie in to the judges?" Lucy asked, interrupting her brother.

"We tried," the youngest Proetz kid said. "But no one's answering. I think we're too far from the last checkpoint, and not close enough to the finish. This is like a dead zone for communication."

"Freddy," Herb said, gesturing to his brother. "Come back here." Herb instructed Freddy to stand on the big brake hook at the back of the Peaches' sled. As soon as Freddy was in Herb's former position, Herb stepped off the back of the sled and said to his siblings, "I think we should help them. I know how to fix their problem—the dogs trust me and will let me untangle them—and I don't feel right about driving away and leaving them out here alone."

"They're not alone," Lucy said. "All the other sleds are going to come this way eventually, and then Philip will zip past on his snowmobile. They'll be fine. Eventually. It's a *race*, Herb."

"I know it's a race," Herb said, his voice soft. "And I know you want to win, Lulu. But I don't think any of us wants to win like *this*."

Freddy glanced at Lucy. "Herb's kind of right."

"Think about it," Herb said. "Even if we stay and help them, maybe we'll still finish fast enough that we can win the Frozen Olympics. If we ditch them, we'll *definitely* win but I don't think I'll ever feel good about it. I won't feel like the Frozen Best if I don't help a fellow team in need. It's not just the Proetzes," he added. "We're also leaving a whole team of dogs out here to get cold and nervous and antsy. It's not right."

"What if Dad had ditched Johan down in the glacial crevasse at the research station?" Freddy blurted out. "He knew he was disappointing and worrying us by not coming back from his research trip when he said he would, but even still, he made the best choice in the moment and did the right thing."

"That's not a fair comparison," Lucy snapped back. "Johan's situation was life-and-death. This is just a slight *setback* for the Proetzes. It's not like they'll *die* out here if we don't help." Neither brother said more. They just looked at her, obviously waiting for her to see this situation from another angle.

Lucy took a deep breath. One of the dogs from the Proetzes' sled dog team looked at her desperately, giving her the saddest puppy-dog-face she'd ever seen. Lucy looked away, turning instead to study the three Proetz kids. They all looked utterly miserable, cold, and angry. She could suddenly imagine how awful it would feel to be in the position they were currently in. She'd always felt like she was a good role model for her younger brothers, but at this moment, they were right:

She wasn't being the kind of person she wanted to be if she left them out here to struggle on their own.

Lucy growled to express her annoyance, then glared at Ellen. "If we help you get your sled going again, do you promise to let us finish ahead of you?"

"Obviously." Ellen narrowed her eyes at Lucy. "But we don't need you to help us. We wouldn't ask that. We can just wait for one of the official people to come by in a while. This *is* a race, you know?"

"Yeah," Lucy grumbled, climbing out of her cozy spot inside their sled. "I know."

While Herb began untangling the dogs' harnesses and ropes, Freddy stayed standing on the back of the Peach sled and Lucy worked with Ellen and her brothers to get their sled back to upright on its tracks. It didn't take long to get the sled back into position, but Herb's work of untangling dogs took a little more time and patience. He'd just gotten the lead dogs sorted out and back in their positions when Freddy called out, "Here come two other sleds!"

Lucy looked over her shoulder and spotted the dad and his two daughters in their fish sled gliding toward them, in the lead. The dad slowed his dog team down and offered to get out and help, but Herb waved them past. He did the same thing when the father-son team from Michigan—who were riding with one of the professional mushers, who fully stopped their sled dog team and offered more help—passed just a minute later. As soon as Herb got the Proetz sled's final dog untangled, the mother-daughter team from Maine sailed past with a wave.

A moment later, Philip zipped up behind the group in his snowmobile. "What's going on here?" he asked loudly, having to yell over the cacophony of two teams of barking and howling dogs.

"The Proetzes had a little problem," Herb said. "But I think we got it all sorted out now."

Philip sent Herb back to his own sled and took over, offering to help the Proetz kids get settled into their sled and make sure they made it to the finish line safely. "See you back at the kennel," he said, waving the Peaches off.

By the time Herb gave the Peach sled dog team the command to go, all the other teams who had passed them during their stop to help the Proetzes were long gone. Lucy was frustrated, sad, and disappointed. But even as they glided past the finish line and heard the judges announce over a bullhorn that they'd come in fourth place during that day's race, she knew they'd done the right thing.

FINAL FROZEN OLYMPICS SCORE SHEET

Proetz Family Farm (Montana): 3 3 5 6 ⑥

Seaside B&B (Washington): 2 3 3 3 ⑥

Anderson's Resort (Michigan): 1 1 4 4 ⑥

Cottages in the Middle of Nowhere (Maine):
0 3 3 5 ⑥

Peachtree B&B (Minnesota): 0 2 3 6 ⑥

From the Sketchbook of Freddy Peach:

IDEAS FOR "THEME WEEKENDS" AT THE PEACHTREE B&B

Dogsledding Trips with White Wilderness Sled Dog Adventures

Ice-Carving Competitions

Igloo-Building Contest

Learn to bake pies with Great Aunt Lucinda

Tiny-dog dogsledding races

Food Truck Festival!

Deep Sea Fishing on Lake Superior

Shipwreck Tour

Book Club Weekend Retreat

Rescue Dog Adoption Weekend

Snowshoeing Adventures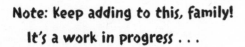

Note: Keep adding to this, family!
 It's a work in progress . . .

22

THE FINAL CURTAIN

Freddy stood at the edge of the stage in the Frozen Globe theater later that night, waiting for his cue to go on. Oystein was standing beside him and must have sensed Freddy's nerves, since he placed one of his massive, paw-like hands on Freddy's shoulder and squeezed— the squeeze was just hard enough that Freddy was a little surprised his shoulder hadn't been pulled off by the friendly gesture.

Just as the scene before theirs wrapped up onstage, Freddy double-checked the belt on his costume pants and put his hand on the hilt of his prop (but still very real) sword. It was finally showtime!

As the crowd of actors who were in Freddy's scene rushed onto the stage for their battle, he let himself get caught up in the moment and forced himself *not* to look out into the audience. He already knew Dad, Lucy, Herb, and Great Aunt Lucinda were in the front row, since Anna had told him that when she warned him before "curtain" that he better not break character and smile at his family during the show. "You're one of us," she reminded him. "A professional. You need to remember that part of our job in theater is to transport our guests to another place and time; but to do that, you need to be able to transport yourself. So even though your family is going to be almost close enough to touch, you have to forget they're there for a bit."

Freddy heard what she was saying, and though it was almost impossible not to grin at Herb, or wave his sword for Dad, or let Great Aunt Lucinda see him tug at the dirty-looking wig they'd put him in for the performance, or yell out someone else's line to impress Lucy, he stayed in character. He'd never want to forget that his family was there supporting him, but he could *pretend* for a few minutes, at least. By some miracle, Freddy remembered his choreography, too, and only took one misstep that caused him to land his sword against Oystein's shield in such a way that he thought his arm might vibrate right off his body.

When his one (short) battle scene was over, Freddy waited and watched the rest of the show from a tucked-away corner of the wing backstage. While he'd loved watching the performance from the audience with his dad a few nights earlier (Anna had been right; Freddy clearly hadn't ever tried watching the right *kind* of theater to get him interested!), he'd already decided that being part of the group behind the scenes was even better. He loved getting a totally different view of the action onstage, and especially enjoyed being part of all the hustle and work and little details that had to happen between scenes to keep the audience sucked in.

Once, Lucy had mentioned that there was a tech crew and a set-building team for the middle school theater shows. Next year, when he was in sixth grade, he just might need to check that out. He wasn't sure *acting* was necessarily his thing (unless there were always fake swords and armor involved), but he was starting to realize that being a part of a theatrical world was pretty amazing. Building sets would maybe be a little bit like building their summer cardboard fortress at Cardboard Camp, he reasoned, and that was his favorite week of the year; if he could extend that fun to *more* weeks of the year, all the better.

After the show, Freddy invited his family into the tiny backstage area so they could touch and hold some of the props and weapons and meet a few of the other actors. Great Aunt Lucinda somehow charmed one of the stage managers to let her try on a giant velvet gown and heavy jeweled crown she spotted somewhere backstage. "I want to wear a costume, too!" Herb hollered out in his most charming voice, and before long, all five Peaches were suited up in furs and vests and armor and a whole collection of things that Anders and Anna and a few other members of the cast and crew dug up for them.

Freddy couldn't think of a more perfect ending to a perfect trip . . . until later that night, when the end of their trip got even *better.* After spending their second-to-last night of the trip in the warm hotel, Freddy had decided he absolutely must spend his final night in The Under the Sea Suite, since he and Lucy hadn't yet tried that one out . . . and he didn't want Lucy to go home without getting a turn in her favorite room. Herb decided he wanted to bunk with Great Aunt Lucinda in the warm hotel again, and Dad declared that after spending a whole night out on a glacier he would *never* sleep on ice again. But before Freddy and his sister tucked into their frozen suite for one final night on ice, they were all summoned to the Icehotel's Ice Bar for one final meeting with all the other sweepstakes winners.

As he and his siblings entered the Ice Bar with their

dad and Great Aunt Lucinda, Freddy nearly bumped into the three Proetz kids. Ellen stepped aside to let the Peaches go in first and flashed what Freddy thought might be a smile in their direction.

"Great job today," Freddy said. "And the rest of the week."

"Yeah," Ellen said quietly. "You too." Then, just as the Peaches were walking away, she called out, "I hope you win Frozen Best. You deserve it."

Freddy and Lucy both spun around. "Thanks." Freddy still couldn't believe that the final score of the Frozen Olympics had ended up with each team finishing with six total points. But that's what had happened, based on the order they finished in that afternoon's sled dog race. The sled design competition would be used as a tiebreaker.

"Your family was fun to compete against," Freddy told her. "It's been great meeting you all."

"Yeah," Ellen said. "You too. And I—" Her brother Finn nudged her with his elbow, making Ellen cringe. She went on. "I wanted to say that I'm sorry I haven't been very nice to you this week. I just really like to win, and sometimes it makes me act—"

"Like a jerk," Finn said, cutting Ellen off. She shot him a nasty look. "She's actually a pretty cool sister, most of the time. But when she's got her game face on, look out. Ellen Proetz is fierce."

"I'm not sure I've been my best this week, either, and I'm sorry for that," Lucy said. "Friends from now on?"

While they waited for the other sweepstakes winners to arrive, the Proetz and Peach families sat together, all chatting and laughing about some of the strangest guests and customers the Proetz family had met during their years running the Proetz Family Farm, and then the Peaches entertained them with stories of some of the crazy customers *they'd* met during their food truck adventure the past summer.

The evening continued to get even better when Josef, Lo, and Anders came in and announced that the Peaches had been chosen as the Frozen Best. Apparently, all four of the other teams had talked to the judges and insisted that the Peaches deserved to win, since they'd only lost their lead in the dogsledding race because they'd stopped to help a fellow team in need. But then Anders announced that even *without* the other teams' support, the judges had already determined that the peach pie sled design was everyone's favorite. To make the win even sweeter, Josef told them *he* would get to be part of the Icehotel team who would be sent to visit them in Minnesota next winter to help build the miniature Ice

Castle in the Peach Pit's backyard. Freddy couldn't wait to welcome him to Minnesota!

❦ ❦ ❦

The next morning, all the Peaches had to wake up extra early to finish packing, grab some breakfast, and catch their van ride to the Kiruna airport for the first of their three flights home. As he dumped his warm gear in the equipment room for the last time, Freddy was groggy and bleary-eyed and very sad to see their family's latest Great Peach Adventure come to a close. But the week at the Icehotel had been a total success, and Freddy couldn't wait to test out some of the fun ideas he'd gotten for The Peachtree B&B this week.

Just as they were dumping their mittens and snowsuits onto the counter to be laundered for the next guests who would use them, Josef came rushing into the equipment room. "Peach kids!" he said, breathless. "Suit back up."

"We need to get a move on," Dad said, checking his watch. "Our flight leaves in three hours, and they ask that we be at the airport two hours early."

"I promise I'll have them there in plenty of time," Josef said, grinning. "Dad and Great Aunt Peach, you'll join the family luggage in the van. Lo is going to drive you there soon. But Herb, Freddy, and Lucy, I have a little surprise for you. Come along."

All three Peach kids threw their warm gear back on and followed Josef outside. There, two teams of dogs were waiting, along with two sleds and Philip. "We thought you might like to take a special ride to the airport this morning," Philip told them. "All of your friends at the Icehotel want to give our Frozen Best family a happy send-off."

"Do we—" Herb shrieked. "Do we get to ride with the *dogs* to the airport?" Freddy knew Herb was having a hard time leaving all his new furry friends behind. One last ride on a dogsled would surely help soothe the sting of saying goodbye.

"Indeed you do," Philip said, laughing his big, Santa-like laugh. Freddy really hoped someday he would be able to grow a beard like Philip's!

The teams of sled dogs barked to show their impatience to get moving. As soon as they were loaded up in their sled, Herb and Philip's team of dogs began to run with Lucy nestled happily into the riding compartment. All the dogs went silent the moment they were given permission to set off down the snowy path alongside the road that led to the Kiruna airport.

A moment later, Freddy and Josef hopped onto the

back of the other sled. With one final glance back over his shoulder at the majestic ice palace they'd been lucky enough to call home for the past week, Freddy thought about something he'd begun to realize over the course of this latest family adventure: It wasn't good luck that had helped turn their lives around this past year, but rather, the choices they'd made that had led to some very good things. He knew the hurt and sadness of the past few years would never disappear, but for a family like the Peaches, Freddy had a hunch that things would keep getting better . . . no luck required. (Of course, a *little* luck would always be appreciated!)

"All right!" Freddy cried, giving his dogs the command to run down the bright, sparkling, snowy path after his siblings and their sled. Then he pumped his fist in the air and called out, "Peach power!"

FROZEN BEST!!!

AUTHOR'S NOTE

About twenty-five years ago, while I was living and studying in Sweden for one amazing year, I got to spend a single night sleeping inside the real Icehotel. Even at the time, I knew it was a once-in-a-lifetime experience, and ever since that visit, I've been trying to find the perfect book in which to use this once-in-a-lifetime setting. Before I finished writing the first book in The Great Peach Experiment series, I had already devised my plan to get the Peaches to Sweden in Book 3—and luckily, my editors were on board with the plan!

Please be aware that I took *major* liberties with my fictionalized version of this real-world setting, and I'm certain the actual Icehotel and its surroundings don't even remotely resemble the place I've created in this book. But by looking back on pictures from my own

visit and pulling out memories of that frozen adventure years ago, I hope I was able to accurately convey some of the feelings one might experience on a trip to this kind of magical, icy wonderland. I created a world and town around the Icehotel that worked for the story I wanted to tell in this book, and I'll be honest: Most of it is totally made up. But I did base a few things in *Frozen Peaches* on real stuff I got to experience during my visit there many years ago (the existence of a Frozen Globe theater, the Ice Bar and its carved-ice glasses, the borrowed snowsuits that made me feel like a walking marshmallow, the little red church poking out of the snow in the middle of nowhere, among many other things). And it's a fact that the hotel melts and gets redesigned and rebuilt from scratch each year.

The little glacial research center Walter Peach visits in this book is also loosely based on a real-life place:

Tarfala Research Station, which is a field station for Stockholm University. My husband (who has his PhD in Paleoclimate, which means he studied many of the same things as Walter Peach—soil; ocean cores; climate change; and fancy, important stuff like that) had a chance to study there many years ago, and his stories and pictures of the beautiful setting and glacial crevasses he saw during that trip still hang on our walls to this day. The real research station is not actually located just a short dogsled-ride away from the Icehotel, but for the purposes of this book, I dropped a loose version of the station right where I needed it, to make it work for this story.

I often say that the best part of writing fiction is that you get to make stuff up. Try it, friends. It's fun!

Special thanks to Heather, Taylor, Peter, and all the dogs at White Wilderness Sled Dog Adventures, for showing me and my family the basics of dogsledding and letting us try it out. That was, by far, some of the best research I've *ever* gotten to do for a book! Also, thanks to many of my Swedish and Norwegian friends—Anna, Anders, Josef, Philip, Lo, Gunnar, Johan, Oystein, and Eline (and Katia, who is not Swedish, but was a friend of mine *in* Sweden and therefore got a shout-out as one of the researchers)—whose names I stole for this book. I loved filling this Icehotel world with some of my favorite Scandinavian friends!

LOOK FOR THE FOURTH
GREAT PEACH ADVENTURE:

DUCK, DUCK, PEACH!

While her brothers got to work on their end-of-year homework and projects and continued to dig for snacks in the kitchen, Lucy raced upstairs to survey their collection of guest rooms to see what would need to get done before people began to arrive in town for the Festival of Ships.

They had three guest suites at the Peachtree B&B, and Lucy loved each one for a different reason. But her absolute favorite guest room was the one she herself had designed—The Winter Suite, which was decorated to look like a winter wonderland all year long. Before the Peaches had moved into the mansion, the house (and dogs) had belonged to their Great Aunt Lucinda, whose favorite holiday was Christmas. In fact, she loved Christmas so much that she'd even named her four little "treasures" (aka the dogs) after four of Santa's reindeer: Dasher, Rudolph, Donner, and Vixen.

The rooms were all fairly tidy, and each had fresh sheets on the beds, but every guest suite smelled a little stale and in two of them, a fine layer of dust had settled over the dressers, desks, and bed frames. The Peaches kept all the guest room doors closed when no one was staying there, so the dogs couldn't sneak in and leave any smelly or wet "treasures" of their own on the floors or beds in the guest suites. Dog messes were not exactly a warm way to welcome visitors to a bed-and-breakfast.

Lucy quickly dusted each of the rooms and took an inventory of some of the things that would be needed for their guests. They'd have to get more shampoo, and probably make welcome baskets with local snacks and drinks, and maybe she could even leave a little rubber duck on each pillow in the guest rooms to celebrate the reason they were all in town: the Festival of Ships and the introduction of the World's Largest Rubber Duck!

For the first time in her life, Lucy was feeling excited to see the school year come to an end. As much as she loved school (seventh grade had been great!), she couldn't wait to see what the first week of summer would bring, with a full house for the first time ever and all kinds of interesting people in town for such a unique event. After a topsy-turvy couple of years filled with fun trips and unusual family experiments, this summer would certainly set the stage for the next chapter in the Peaches' lives as their lives began to settle into something a little closer to normal.

That is, as normal as life could be with a magician lurking around the backyard, the World's Largest Rubber Duck bobbing around in the harbor down the hill, a food truck festival to organize, a lake packed full of strange and unique ships, a house full of naughty dogs, and a family like the Peaches . . . whose definition of normal usually tended to be just a bit different from the rest of the world's.

ERIN SODERBERG DOWNING has written more than fifty books for kids, tweens, and young adults, including several series for young readers: The Great Peach Experiment (book one was a Junior Library Guild Gold Standard Selection), Puppy Pirates, and The Quirks. She has also published many other novels for middle-grade readers, including *Moon Shadow* and *Controlled Burn*. Erin's favorite hobbies are reading, swimming, baking, exploring the woods, traveling with her family, and walking around Minneapolis lakes with her fluffy and mischievous dogs, Wally and Nutmeg. More information can be found at ErinSoderberg.com.